Realising and Actualising Your Dreams

Hope Nmerukini Chinwo-Amadi

Dedication

This book is dedicated to God, who has guided me through challenges so that I can share this story. Without Him, I wouldn't be here to tell it.

Table of Content

Acknowledgments

In sincere appreciation and heartfelt gratitude, I extend my deepest thanks to:

God Almighty, for His unfailing love and guidance throughout this journey.

I want to honour my parents who brought me into this world and have been a constant source of strength and inspiration. To my husband and my wonderful precious offspring, whose understanding and encouragement have provided me with the courage to soar to new heights like an eagle. I also want to appreciate my grandchildren who bring so much joy and happiness to my life. I am profoundly grateful for your support.

To all the wonderful mothers whose paths crossed mine during my 25 years in Western Europe, I celebrate you. Special mention goes to the following:

Mrs V. Okeke, you have been a pivotal support system throughout this journey, welcoming me in like a daughter and always being there for me. To Deaconess R. Yakub, it has been a blessing to serve together and I have learnt from your dedication and servant's heart, that I have seen God in you. Yetunde Ayo (Yetty Oremi), thank you for standing by me through thick and thin for over two decades. To Mrs Florence Chinasa Okoro Achibom, thank you for all the things you do for me in my absence - your regular visits to my father means a lot to me.

Mother in Israel - Pastor Mrs Folake Odugbile. I have grown spiritually under your leadership. Your encouragement has been invaluable. Deaconess Elizbeth Hephzibah, you have been a prayer buddy, and your mentorship opened my eyes to how television can sometimes cloud one's vision. Thank you, Mama, for your unconditional love.

Introduction

In the indigenous and culturally rich landscape of beautiful Africa, a young woman named Nkem embarked on a journey filled with hopes and dreams. Raised with a foundation of strong values and aspirations, her path seemed destined for greatness. Yet, despite her upbringing, she found herself dealing with the complexities of life's unfolding story.

In her early twenties, Nkem got caught up in the whirlwind of marriage. But as the layers of married life started to peel away, she was faced with the raw truths of human nature. Each day, the clear vision she had for her future became blurred with doubt and uncertainty.

What she once thought were stable pillars of life and marriage turned out to be filled with challenges. The foundations, built on fleeting emotions and misplaced pride, began to crumble under the weight of unmet expectations. Nkem found herself battling feelings of inadequacy and disappointment as she tried to navigate her new life.

This is a story of self-discovery and finding one's true purpose. Nkem's journey is a reminder of how complex relationships can be, and the constant search for meaning and fulfilment.

At the core of this story is the importance of realising one's dreams. Personal growth and understanding who you are stand out as key themes. From a young age, Nkem faced challenges to her sense of worth and ambition, especially as a woman from her community.

She recalls her father's words, which seemed to limit her potential and reserve education for her brother. However, her strong sense of purpose drove her to defy these expectations. Refusing to settle for apprenticeships in the food industry, she pursued a path driven by her desire for more.

Reflecting on her journey, she emphasises the importance of aligning purpose with action. She recounts her decision to pursue education against familial wishes, a bold stride towards her envisioned future. Her story underscores the Biblical saying: "Faith without works is dead," stressing the significance of proactive steps towards realising one's aspirations.

This book challenges prevailing beliefs of dependency, particularly among women and encourages self-empowerment. The primary focus is on empowering female figures to stand out and pursue their aspirations with unshakeable confidence and determination. While the audience extends to both men and women, the story is particularly geared towards inspiring women to take charge of their destinies and embrace their potential.

The story offers valuable insights into the importance of seeking divine guidance and surrendering one's plans and purposes to God. Through personal stories and reflections, readers are encouraged to place their trust in God as the author of their lives, recognising that His timing and plans transcend human understanding.

Central to the book's message is the view of self-reliance and self-belief. Rather than waiting for others to pave the way, readers are urged to take proactive steps towards their goals, guided by faith in God's providence. The narrative emphasises the inborn worth of every individual, reminding readers that they are not in competition with others but rather on a unique journey ordained by God.

Ultimately, the book serves as a ray of hope and encouragement for women seeking to realise their dreams and fulfil their God-given purpose.

CHAPTER 1

Growing Up Experiences

The sky loomed a heavy grey as the rain battered down on the village. Each drop seemed to match the weight in Nkem's heart. She stood by the window of her family home, watching as the rain turned the red earth into a shiny, slippery mess. The wind howled, but inside, she could hear her father's cheerful laughter from the kitchen, a clear contrast to the storm outside.

Her gaze drifted to a black-and-white photograph of her late brother hanging on the wall. His smile was frozen in time, a reminder of the happiness that had once filled their home. The photograph seemed to speak to her, urging her to think about what lay ahead.

She grew up in a large family, the seventh of eight children, with four sisters and three brothers. Tragedy struck early in her life when she lost one of her brothers who lived abroad at the time, and later, another sister passed away after she got married. This left her with three sisters and two brothers, most of whom were older, except for her youngest sister.

A knock on the door pulled her from her thoughts. She opened it to find her youngest sister, her eyes brimming with excitement. Nkem smiled, remembering how she had fought for her to attend a private primary school. The family had always preferred the local schools, but Nkem strongly advocated for the importance of a better education.

"She's too bright for the village school," Nkem said, determined to make them see her point. It took a while, but her parents eventually agreed, allowing her sister to follow Nkem's path towards higher education. Her sister had done well, proving that Nkem's efforts were worth it.

Now, as her sister stood there, ready to continue her studies, Nkem felt that same sense of determination rising in her again. The road ahead would have its challenges, but Nkem knew her sister was ready. She played a huge role in clearing the way, and now her sister could confidently go forward.

The village was known for its traditional ways, and Nkem always felt out of place. Her family had their expectations, and while they loved and supported her, they couldn't understand her desire for something beyond their simple village life. She had seen her future before her like a clear path, but her heart yearned for a different route, one full of challenges and new beginnings.

As the storm continued, Nkem took a deep breath, her mind racing about what was coming. She knew that the path she was about to choose would not only go against her family's expectations but also test her faith and courage. The road ahead was unclear, filled with both difficulties and exciting possibilities.

She glanced back at the photograph of her brother, feeling both sadness and inspiration. His memory reminded her that life is fleeting and that it is important to follow one's path, no matter how tough it might seem.

Amid the storm, Nkem made a quiet promise to herself. She would not let her fears drown out her dreams. With renewed determination, she turned away from the window, ready to face the challenges and embrace the opportunities that lay ahead.

As she prepared to take her first steps into an uncertain future, the rain began to ease, as if signalling that, like the storm, the obstacles in her way might eventually clear.

Nkem's parents were a remarkable couple. Her father loved her mother deeply, a love that endured until death parted them. He had a passion for cooking and baking, often sharing his creations with the entire family. In his generosity, he gave his wife nearly half of his estate for her upkeep. She was a skilled farmer who sold her crops independently, never accounting for the money to her husband. He, a down-to-earth man who disliked conflict, never questioned her about the proceeds from her sales. Adored by his in-laws for the love and care he showed their sister, he was well respected in the community, while his wife was admired–and even envied by some–for her popularity.

Each month, the family was well-stocked with food, thanks to his company, so there was never any lack. Money was never an issue, yet the couple didn't place as much value on education as they might have.

Nkem's mother was a strong and formidable woman, commanding respect from her children. If they failed to return home on time, she would lock them out, forcing them to seek refuge at their grandmother's house until their father came to fetch them.

Her childhood was typical of village life, spent working on the farm alongside her mother and siblings, fetching water from the stream, and assisting her eldest sister in caring for her baby while missing school for several months. Household chores, such as cooking and laundry, were also part of her routine.

As a teenager, she was lively and full of energy. Many friends surrounded her, and she shared countless happy moments with her best friend, Chi (may her soul rest in peace). The two would play, eat, talk, and laugh together. Nkem shared a close bond with her cousin Agbu, who attended the same secondary school.

Throughout her teenage and young adult years, she enjoyed a large circle of friends. While at the Polytechnic, she was actively involved in a Christian fellowship, serving as the financial secretary. Her life was a whirlwind of activities until her wedding and graduation, which occurred around the same time.

Nkem's parents were both respected in their fields. Her father, with his flair for cooking, was known for his delicious meals and innovative recipes. The kitchen was his domain, and he took great pride in preparing food that brought joy to his family and neighbours. Her mother shared her enthusiasm for her father's culinary arts but also remained deeply connected to her roots as a farmer. She managed a small but productive plot of land, where she grew vegetables and cassava, which often found their way into their family meals.

Despite their lack of formal education, they understood the value of schooling. However, in their village, practical skills and hands-on experience were considered more important than academic achievements. This belief was reflected in the paths chosen by Nkem's two older sisters, who followed their father into the world of catering after finishing secondary school. They quickly established themselves as skilled chefs, much like their father.

Nkem's brothers also chose practical fields, each diverging from the academic route. Her older brother travelled overseas to work. This left the family tradition to be taken over by the girls.

However, Nkem felt a calling that set her apart. One

evening, as her family sat around the dinner table, she shared her decision with them. The kitchen was bustling with the sounds of cooking, pots clattering, and the sizzling of ingredients. The air was filled with the spices of her father's latest dish.

"Dad, Mum," Nkem began, her voice steady but nervous, "I've been thinking a lot about what I want to do with my life."

Her father looked up from his cooking, his face reflecting curiosity and concern. "What's on your mind, Nkem?"

"I don't want to follow the path of becoming a chef," she said, taking a deep breath. "I feel that God has something different planned for me. I want to go to a polytechnic and continue my education."

Her mother, who was serving the food, paused and exchanged a glance with her husband. "But Nkem," she said gently, "you know how important the family business is. Your sisters are doing well, and there's always a place for you in the kitchen."

"I know, Mum," Nkem replied, her voice firm. "I appreciate everything you've done for me, but I feel strongly that I need to pursue this on my own. I believe it's the right path for me."

Her father sighed, his brow wrinkling in thought. "It's not what we expected," he said slowly. "But if this is what you truly believe is best for you, then we'll support your decision."

Nkem's heart swelled with relief and gratitude. She had feared their disappointment, but their acceptance made her feel more determined. "Thank you, Dad. Thank you, Mum."

Later, her father approached her with a serious but kind expression. "I've arranged for you to start an apprenticeship in catering," he said. "It's a good opportunity, and I hope you'll at least give it a try."

Nkem felt a pang of guilt but remained firm. "I appreciate the offer, but I've made up my mind. I need to forge my own path."

With a nod of understanding, her father stepped away, leaving her to reflect on her decision. It was a difficult decision, one that went against the grain of family expectations, but she was determined to forge her own path. In the following weeks, she prepared for her new journey, enrolling in the polytechnic with a blend of excitement and apprehension.

Her decision was uncommon for someone from her family, but she was ready to embrace the challenges ahead. The path she had chosen was different from the one laid out by her family, but it was the one she felt was meant for her.

As Nkem continued her studies, she encountered something that would change her life forever. She met Jesus Christ and experienced a profound transformation. Serving God became a central part of her life, bringing her a deep sense of purpose and joy. However, she sometimes wondered if she should have devoted more time to her faith before stepping into marriage. Despite this, she embraced her journey, knowing that every step she took was part of a larger plan. Her determination to follow her path and pursue education despite her family's expectations was guided by her trust in God. She actively applied scripture in her life, especially Proverbs 3:5-6: "Trust in the Lord with all your heart, And lean not on your own understanding; In all your ways acknowledge Him, And He shall direct your paths."

In high school, Nkem was surrounded by many friends and acquaintances, yet she always felt there was something unique about her that set her apart. She wasn't easily accessible, and people often had to put in effort to get close to her. This wasn't due to arrogance but rather a sense of how God had created her, as a person not easily swayed or casually approached. She liked this about herself; it gave her a sense of worth and made her interactions with others more meaningful.

Nkem's time in school was enjoyable, but not without its challenges. Initially, her parents, particularly her mother, were hesitant about her attending high school. They had other plans for her, perhaps in line with the family tradition. However, she was determined to pursue her education. She ignored their concerns and pressed on with the support of friends and her sister, who was already working by then. With their encouragement, she completed her Ordinary National Diploma (OND) and moved on to gain work experience in an oil company in her state.

This moment was a clear demonstration of God's provision and guidance, proving the promise of Jeremiah 29:11: "For I know the thoughts that I think towards you, says the Lord, thoughts of peace and not of evil, to give you a future and a hope."

As Nkem transitioned from school to adulthood, she faced new challenges to be detailed in the upcoming chapters. Reflecting on her life, she sees how God's mercy has guided her through every challenge. Her journey, though filled with difficulties, has also been marked by the realisation and actualisation of her dreams. This is why this book is titled "Realising and Actualising Your Dreams and Purpose in Life." From a young age, this lady knew that God had a special purpose for her. She pursued that purpose with determination, listened to God's direction and put things in order with God's help. Understanding that each person has a unique purpose is supported by Ephesians 2:10: "For we are His workmanship, created in Christ Jesus for good works, which God prepared beforehand that we should walk in them."

Every person on earth has a unique purpose, a divine calling instilled by God. Your purpose is the gift God has bestowed upon you, a seed planted within your soul. Actualising and realising this purpose is the gift you give to yourself. It requires hard work, integrity, and determination to walk in alignment with your purpose and to see it come to fruition.

As the Bible says in Proverbs 16:3, "Commit your works to the Lord, and your plans will be established." This reminds us that when we dedicate our efforts to God, He will guide us and help us achieve the purpose He has set for us. Walking in your purpose is not always easy, but with faith, persistence, and a steadfast heart, you can unlock the full potential of the life God has designed for you.

CHAPTER 2

Marriage

In today's world, where the true meaning of marriage often gets lost, it's crucial to return to the wisdom that has guided countless couples through the ages. The Bible speaks clearly in Matthew 19:6: "So they are no longer two, but one flesh. Therefore, what God has joined together, let no one separate." This powerful verse doesn't just describe a union; it reveals a divine bond so sacred and unbreakable that it passes human understanding. God Himself ordains marriage, making it as a covenant that we are called to honour, cherish, and protect.

Marriage is not simply a contract between two individuals; it is a covenant where two become one, not two remaining separate or, worse, divided. When approached according to God's Word, marriage is a beautiful and fulfilling relationship. It is a journey that began in the Kingdom of God and should be nurtured and sustained in the presence of God.

The Scriptures provide clear guidelines on how a marriage should be lived and led. These divine principles are not just suggestions; they are the foundation for a strong, loving, and enduring relationship. Following the path laid out in the Word can protect you from unnecessary heartache and pain, guiding you towards a marriage that is honourable and reflective of God's love. Hebrews 13:4 further elaborates on this, stating, "Marriage is honourable among all, and the bed undefiled; but fornicators and adulterers God will judge." This verse highlights the importance of keeping the marriage relationship pure and honourable, warning against the consequences of unfaithfulness and impurity.

How the Couple Met

Before beginning her studies at the polytechnic, Nkem had already met the man who would later become her husband. He was about to embark on a career that would take him abroad, and they met just a year before he left. Despite the brief time they spent together, she was certain that he was the one she wanted to marry when the time was right.

Nkem had been invited to a harvest ceremony by her friend Chi. The event took place in her maternal hometown, where her mother was originally from. When she attended the service, she noticed Eme, who was part of the choir. As she danced up to the altar to make her offering of Thanksgiving, Eme and the choir were also dancing and watching her.

At the end of the service, Eme rushed to Chi and said, "I saw your friend. I really like her." He started making an effort to speak with Nkem. Although they exchanged a brief 'hello', Nkem left with Chi and then went to her maternal home. The following day was the bazaar, held right after the Thanksgiving harvest.

Chi later told Nkem that Eme was interested in her and hoped they could become friends. On the evening of the bazaar, Chi took Nkem to Eme's family home. They visited with Eme, his friends, and younger siblings before heading back to the bazaar. During the bazaar, Eme continued to bid loudly on various items, which Chi pointed out to Nkem. She thought to herself that Eme seemed quite handsome.

After the bazaar, the couple had a brief conversation. The next day, while Nkem was fetching water from a public tap, she saw Eme waiting for a bike to take him to the next junction. He stopped to chat with her and invited her to visit him at his office during the week. At that time, mobile phones were not common, and people mostly relied on landlines, which were rare in their area.

Nkem started visiting Eme at his bank office during his breaks, and they would go out for lunch together. They continued to see each other, and every time he went to the village, he would let Chi know, who then informed Nkem. Their relationship grew from there, and they began dating. They liked each other a lot, and their relationship blossomed, leading to the deep connection they shared.

Proverbs 18:22 says, "He who finds a wife finds a good thing, and obtains favour from the Lord." This verse speaks to the sacred and treasured nature of marriage, where a wife is not just a partner but a blessing, a source of joy, and a reflection of God's favour upon a man's life. In the context of this relationship, this verse holds significant meaning.

For Eme, finding Nkem was more than just meeting a woman he wanted to marry; it was an encounter with God's favour. The Scripture emphasises that a wife is a "good thing," a gift from God that brings completeness and joy to a man's life. A woman's presence in a man's life represents a divine blessing, a sign that God is pleased and wants to enrich their lives with love and companionship.

The "good thing" in this verse is not just about the

physical presence of a wife but encompasses all that she brings into a man's life like love, support, wisdom, and partnership. In finding her, Eme was not just gaining a wife; he was gaining a partner who would stand by him through life's trials and triumphs. She would be his confidant, his support system, and the one who would nurture their family with love and care.

In addition, the verse highlights that in finding a wife, a man "obtains favour from the Lord." This phrase suggests that marriage is a channel through which God's favour flows into a person's life. It implies that the union between a husband and wife is blessed by God, and through this relationship, they can experience His grace and favour in abundance. For this couple, it meant stepping into a new level of divine favour, where their relationship would be guided and blessed by God's hand. However, in order for the favour to really work, the foundations need to be right according to Psalm 11:3: "If the foundations are destroyed, what can the righteous do?"

Planning The Registry

The couple began planning their wedding, and they were filled with excitement and anticipation. They had already gone through the introduction ceremony with Nkem's family, and their next step was to register their marriage at the local registry office. Both of them had agreed that this was an important part of their marriage process, a formal step that would solidify their union before the traditional and church ceremonies.

One afternoon, Nkem and Eme visited the registry in their city and completed the necessary paperwork. They returned home feeling accomplished, but that feeling was short-lived. When they shared their plans with Eme's older brother, who had taken on the role of a father figure since their own father had passed away, they were met with resistance. Eme's brother strongly advised against the registry, insisting that it was unnecessary since they were already planning to have both a traditional and church wedding.

Nkem was taken aback. She knew that the registry was a crucial step in making their marriage legally binding, and she couldn't understand why he would dismiss it so casually, especially since he had gone through the same process for his own marriage. Despite his brother's objections, Nkem felt strongly that they should proceed with the registry. She told Eme firmly that if they didn't do the registry, there would be no marriage. For her, they needed to do things properly from the start.

That evening, tensions rose between the couple. After a heated discussion, Nkem left Eme's house and returned to her family home, clearly upset. Her mother, noticing her distress, asked what had happened. She explained the situation, expressing her frustration with his sudden change of heart due to his brother's influence. Her mother listened carefully and then offered her advice. She suggested that if he was not ready to make decisions on his own and was easily swayed by others, perhaps her daughter should reconsider the marriage. Alternatively, her mother offered to speak with Eme's uncle in the village, someone who might have a stronger influence on him and his family.

Following her mother's advice, Nkem decided to visit Eme's uncle. She explained the situation to him, detailing their plans to register the marriage and how Eme's brother had opposed it. The uncle, who worked with the local council, was surprised by the brother's stance. He assured her that the registry was an important step and that it should not be dismissed. He promised to help by arranging a date for them to register their marriage at his council office, but he also expressed a desire to speak with Eme directly.

Feeling a bit more reassured, Nkem returned home. That evening, Eme visited her, and her mother took the chance to speak with him directly. She explained that while she appreciated his love for her daughter, it was essential for him to stand firm in his decisions and not allow his brother or anyone else to dictate what was best for him and Nkem. She pointed out that if he and Nkem had already agreed on something as important as registering their marriage, he should not change his mind just because his brother disagreed.

Eme, visibly uncomfortable, tried to explain that his brother wasn't against the marriage but simply saw the registry as redundant since they were having other ceremonies. However, Nkem's mother was firm. She reminded him that he needed to be decisive and consider her feelings and the promises they had made to each other.

Realising the gravity of the situation, he apologised for the confusion and assured them that he was committed to the marriage. He suggested they visit his uncle together, as the uncle had requested, to finalise the plans for the registry. The next day, Nkem and Eme travelled to the village to meet with the uncle, who reiterated his support for their decision to register the marriage and expressed his disappointment in Eme's brother for trying to interfere. With the uncle's backing, it was decided that they would proceed with the registry as planned.

This experience, so early in their marriage journey, was a clear sign to Nkem of the challenges that lay ahead. It highlighted the importance of standing firm in their decisions as a couple and the need for clear communication, especially when external influences threatened to disrupt their plans.

Court Wedding

Eme's uncle arranged for a new date at a different council, and the couple went ahead and completed the registry. With that done, he returned to Europe, and she was left to reflect on the many changes and challenges that had already begun to emerge in their relationship.

She was young and inexperienced, unaware of the complexities that life and marriage could bring. Over time, she began to notice things that didn't quite add up. He would send her money from Europe, and she would go to the bank to collect it. However, on one particular day, the cashier informed her that the information she provided didn't match what was in their system. Confused, she left the bank and went to make a phone call to him. When she explained the situation to him, he gave her a different name to use for collecting the money. He instructed her to always use this new name whenever he sent money, but he didn't explain why. Naive and trusting, she didn't question it further and continued to collect money under this name, unaware of the deeper implications.

As their wedding day approached, more issues arose. Nkem had made preparations for the traditional and church weddings, but there was always some tension and confusion. One evening, Eme's siblings called a meeting to discuss the wedding plans. Nkem and her friend were left waiting in the car for hours while the men held their meeting inside. When she was finally called in, she was asked about the progress of the wedding plans on the side of her family. She assured them that everything was in order for the traditional marriage, which had been organised by her parents.

Despite the challenges, the couple continued with their wedding preparations. They went shopping for the things they needed, but the stress of the situation often led to arguments between them. The short time frame for planning, along with the lack of support from others, made everything more difficult. However, they managed to complete the traditional marriage, and the church wedding was the next big event.

Wedding Day

The night of the wedding, the bride-to-be did not sleep with anticipation. The sun had barely risen on Nkem and Eme's wedding day, but already it seemed that the day's plans were in jeopardy. Nkem awoke with a lot of excitement, her heart racing at the thought of marrying the love of her life. She could picture the beautiful church, the smiles of her friends and family, and the life she and Eme were about to start together.

However, as she and her parents prepared to leave for the church, a sudden blow of misfortune struck. The car that was supposed to take them to the church refused to start. Panic set in as they realised the car was completely broken down, and the wedding clock was ticking away. Each passing minute seemed to pull them further away from their dream day.

Nkem and her parents stood by the roadside in their wedding clothes, looking out of place in the middle of all the chaos. They were trying hard to get help, but each time they tried to find a different car, things just got worse. What was meant to be an exciting day quickly turned into worry as they feared being late.

After what felt like a very long time, Nkem's second cousin arrived in his car. He had come to the house to check if everyone had left, and found his uncle and aunt still waiting. Thankfully, he was able to give Nkem and her parents a lift to the church. Even though the delay had spoiled the grand entrance they had imagined, they were relieved to finally be on their way.

When they arrived at the church, the surprises didn't stop. The bouquet that Nkem had so eagerly awaited had not made it to the church. Instead of the pretty arrangement she had imagined, an auntie had managed to find a quick replacement which was a bouquet that, though kind and thoughtful, was not quite what she had dreamed of. It felt like another piece of her perfect day slipping through her fingers.

Inside the church, things went well. But during the wedding reception, the troubles started again. There were no glasses for the couple to make their toast, which was frustrating. It felt like such a small but important detail had been forgotten, and the bride looked around, hoping for something to make the day feel like the perfect dream she had imagined.

Despite all the chaos and mishaps, the ceremony went ahead. As Nkem and Eme stood before their loved ones, exchanging vows, they were surrounded by the warmth and love of those who had gathered to witness their union. Though the day was not flawless, it was real and memorable, filled with unexpected challenges that made their story unique.

Nkem realised that the imperfections of the day had woven themselves into the fabric of their lives. They became part of their journey. The wedding was chaotic, could this have been a sign that the marriage was also going to be hectic? The wedding might not have been the picture-perfect event she had imagined, but it was their own special day, marked by the joy of their commitment and the support of those who cared for them.

After the wedding, the reality of married life began to set in. Nkem soon realised that the challenges they faced during the wedding planning were just the beginning. As she navigated this new chapter of her life, she often reflected on the choices she had made and the difficulties that lay ahead. Despite everything, she remained committed to making her marriage work, even as she learned that the road ahead would not be easy.

CHAPTER 3

Experiences After Marriage

The day of the Thanksgiving celebration at Eme's family home was supposed to be a joyful occasion, but for Nkem, it was filled with mixed emotions. The house was full of people, laughter, and food, but she felt uneasy as they prepared to leave.

As they returned home, Eme's sister handed Nkem a small, white baby bath. With a mysterious look, she said, "Today and tomorrow."

Nkem was confused. *Why was she given a baby bath?* She

thought. She wasn't the one giving birth. She thanked Eme's sister politely, but the gift made her feel uncomfortable and unsure.

Back in the house, Nkem tried to ignore her feelings, but the gift left her feeling anxious about what lay ahead. The strange present felt like a hint of the difficulties she might face in her new life with Eme.

Two weeks later, while Nkem was at home with a friend, another incident occurred that would mark the beginning of an unsettled marriage. That morning, she prepared yam pepper soup for breakfast. In her family, the yam was served separately from the pepper soup, with palm oil on the side. However, when she brought the meal to the table, he was outraged. In front of her friend, he began shouting about the way she had served the food. Nkem's friend couldn't help but laugh, but for Nkem, the moment was humiliating. Eme took the yam back to the kitchen, mixed it with the oil the way he preferred, and then returned to the table. They ate in silence, but the incident lingered in her mind, a sign of deeper issues in their relationship.

Detained

The situation grew worse when Nkem travelled to meet Eme in Europe. At the airport, she was detained because the passport she was using was not genuine. The customs officials placed her in a facility for asylum seekers, and she was forced to appear in court to request asylum. Eme had to come and collect her, and they finally began their life together in Europe. But this was not the life she had envisioned. She realised she had been smuggled into another country under the guise of marriage, a realisation that filled her with regret and shame.

Once in Europe, Eme instructed his wife to use the same fake passport to apply for a National Insurance number so she could start working. When she arrived at the office, the officials quickly recognised that the passport was not authentic. Nkem and Eme fled the office in a panic, narrowly avoiding further legal trouble. Despite this, Eme continued to obtain false documents from various sources, enabling his wife to stay in the country temporarily. But these documents were flimsy at best, and when her initial one-year residency permit expired, they were unable to provide the necessary birth certificate and other documents required to renew her stay. By this time, Nkem was already pregnant, adding another layer of stress to their risky situation.

Throughout these trials, Nkem maintained her faith and continued to serve God as best she could. However, Eme's financial troubles only added to their difficulties; he had fallen into debt after being duped in a business deal by a man who lacked legal residency in the country. Eme had borrowed money from the bank and from friends, including some of the locals, to fund this ill-fated venture. When the scheme fell apart, he was left with nothing but debt. He hadn't even told her about these financial troubles. The situation had reached a point where he could no longer face the friends he had borrowed money from, and he had strained his relationships with those who might have been able to help him.

One day, while Nkem was still adjusting to her new life, one of Eme's business partners called the house. She answered the phone, and the man on the other end was surprised to learn that she had recently arrived. After a brief conversation, Nkem passed the phone to Eme. The moment the call ended, this man called another one of Eme's friends and told him that Eme had used the borrowed money to travel back home for a lavish wedding. This news spread among his friends, further damaging his reputation.

The tension between Nkem and Eme had been bubbling beneath the surface for weeks, but it reached a boiling point as they drove through the quiet streets towards the home of one of Eme's friends. The crisp air and the glow of streetlights outside did little to ease her mounting unease.

As they approached the friend's house, his expression was unusually tense. He glanced at her with a mix of urgency and unease. "I need you to do something before we get there," he said, his voice unsteady.

Nkem looked at him with a puzzled frown. "What is it?"

He reached over and gently took her hand, his eyes avoiding hers. "I need you to take off your wedding ring," he said quietly. "We haven't told anyone about our marriage yet. We're going to pretend we're still engaged."

Nkem's heart sank. She had hoped that meeting his friends would be a moment of warmth and acceptance. Instead, she felt a cold wave of confusion and hurt wash over her. She had envisioned their visit as a chance to share their happiness, but now it seemed to be shrouded in secrecy and deceit.

With trembling hands, Nkem removed her wedding ring and slipped it into her purse. The simple act felt like a weight lifting off her finger but sinking heavily into her heart. She tried to ignore the pang of betrayal and the growing sense of isolation that this request from Eme triggered. She was doing her best to submit to her husband, as the Bible instructed, but this act of obedience only deepened her feelings of isolation and betrayal.

As they reached the friend's house, the warm glow from the windows and the sounds of laughter from inside seemed to mock her inner turmoil. He smiled and greeted his friends with a casual ease that contrasted sharply with the strained atmosphere in the car. He introduced Nkem as his fiancée, a role she had once been eager to embrace but now found herself struggling to accept.

Nkem put on a brave face, greeting everyone with a smile that didn't quite reach her eyes. She was doing her best to follow his lead, to blend into the role he had assigned her, but each moment spent in this pretence only deepened her feelings of loneliness. The secrecy was a constant reminder of the trust she had placed in him and the growing gap between her expectations and the reality of their marriage.

As the evening progressed, Nkem felt like a shadow in the background, her presence overshadowed by the deception that had been forced upon her. The laughter and friendship around her were a stark contrast to the isolation she felt. She wanted to reach out, to share her true self and her reality, but felt constrained by the role he had imposed.

This night was meant to be a bridge to his world, instead it highlighted the distance between them. Nkem's heart ached with each passing moment, struggling to reconcile her commitment to her husband with the growing disappointment of their marriage. She left the friend's house with a heavy heart, the weight of her ringless finger a painful symbol of the divide that had grown between her and the life she had once envisioned.

As time passed, Nkem began to resist Eme's demands. She started to question the decisions he made, especially when they didn't benefit the family or even himself. However, this newfound assertiveness was met with hostility. Eme accused Nkem of being rebellious, of not respecting or obeying him as a wife should. The more Nkem pushed back, the more Eme tried to paint her as the bad person in their relationship.

When their first child was born, the couple's strained relationship became more evident. A family friend, Afuka came to visit them and entered their bedroom to see the new baby. As she looked around the room, her eyes landed on a wedding photo. The friend was quick to notice but chose not to comment directly. Instead, she simply said, "What a beautiful wedding photo." Eme, caught off guard, could only stammer a vague response. He had never told this friend that they were married, only that they were engaged. The friend didn't press further, but the awkwardness of the moment hung in the air, this was evidence of the secrets and lies that had become a part of Nkem's life.

Despite all this, the friend remained in their lives, continuing to support them in her own way. But for Nkem, these encounters were constant reminders of the instability of her situation, the deception that had brought her to Europe, and the increasingly toxic marriage she was now trapped in.

Nkem's Journey Through a Stormy Marriage

As time went on, Nkem's residency problems worsened. She confronted Eme, telling him that their situation was unsustainable. She suggested that they either relocate to another country and do things properly or that she should return home, allowing him to later come for her officially as his wife. Eme agreed, but things took another turn when someone suggested that there was a country in Europe where having a baby could secure residency. She was already pregnant at that time and was willing to try, but the plan quickly fell apart when Eme failed to pay a woman whose passport they planned to use. At the airport, Nkem was caught with the stolen passport and detained. With her 14-month-old son by her side and his passport in hand, the immigration officers were able to trace their journey.

The officials concluded that she was running away from her husband, and considering her pregnancy, they decided to send her back to where she came from instead of pressing charges. During these trials, she held on to Psalm 46:1, "God is our refuge and strength, a very present help in trouble." It was a reminder that, despite the chaos, she was not alone.

Electricity Cut Off

One particular day, after attending her language class, which she did twice a week, Nkem returned to the house. It was late spring, and the weather was still bright and pleasant, though the afternoon was getting late. As she stepped inside, a strange beeping noise immediately caught her attention. Confused, she glanced around but couldn't pinpoint the source. Deciding to get some water, she opened the fridge, only to realise the power was out.

Concerned, Nkem checked all the appliances in the house, but nothing worked. The entire house had lost electricity. She tried to use the phone, but it was plugged into the mains and was dead as well. Standing there, feeling a mix of confusion and helplessness, she took her son out of the buggy and placed him on a chair. Then she grabbed her mobile and tried calling Eme, repeatedly. His phone rang, but there was no answer – he was likely at work, unaware of the situation.

With no way of resolving the issue on her own, Nkem

called a family friend, explaining what had happened. The friend and his wife reassured her, saying, "Don't worry, someone will come to check the problem. It's still daylight, so you don't need to panic." Their calm words provided some comfort, but Nkem still felt anxious.

She also called her older brother, who was living somewhere else in Europe. After explaining what had happened, her brother sighed and said, "Baby sister, I don't know what to tell you. I never fully supported this marriage, but now that you're here, married and in Europe, there's not much I can do. I will, however, get in touch with your husband and tell him to sort this out." Her brother ended the call after saying that, leaving her feeling even more isolated.

At that moment, Nkem broke down in tears. She wondered how her life had come to this. Despite her sadness, she pulled herself together, fed her son, and waited until their family friend arrived to take them to his home for the evening. Grateful for the support, she packed a few things for herself and her son and stayed with the family for a few days.

Later that week, she went to church, which was near their friend's house. After the service, she spoke to her pastor about the situation. He reassured her, telling her that her husband had already been in touch and that they were working on restoring the electricity. He asked if she and her son were alright, and Nkem assured him they were fine, though her frustration lingered.

As time passed, their marriage continued to be a source of pain and hardship. Despite her efforts to show that all was well for the sake of their children, the constant betrayals, lies, and financial struggles took a toll on her mental health. She battled silently with the sorrow and disappointment that had come to define her marriage. Yet, through it all, she remained resilient, finding strength in her faith and her determination to provide a better life for her children.

1 Corinthians 2:9, says, "But as it is written: 'Eye has not seen, nor ear heard, nor have entered into the heart of man the things which God has prepared for those who love Him.'" At the time, Nkem struggled to understand this

verse, but looking back at her journey from her non-English-speaking country to an English-speaking one, she could see the truth in it.

The transition had not been easy. She remembered returning to Africa with her two children to serve the nation, though she had intended to focus on service. Her residence permit had not been renewed, and she needed to sort things out. When she arrived home, she found that the house she and Eme had rented before their marriage had been occupied by Chris (Eme's cousin) and his new wife. They had moved into the house while she was away, and the rent was due for renewal.

Financial difficulties were a challenge, and Eme even had to take a farm job to help cover the rent. Nkem, who was pregnant at the time, helped with the farm work, picking asparagus while he did the harvesting. One of his friends, after seeing this, expressed his surprise at him bringing his pregnant wife to work on the farm, though he had a European nationality and was doing a regular job.

When Nkem returned home with her children, Chris refused to move out of the house as promised, even though Eme had asked him to. Instead, Chris and his wife remained, and Nkem and her children had to share the accommodation. Chris's wife was never hospitable, failing to offer any meals or a warm welcome. Nkem felt increasingly frustrated with the situation.

One memorable incident was when her children were watching TV, and Chris's wife angrily demanded the remote control. When Nkem intervened, she advised the woman to be kind to the children, as she would one day be a mother herself.

Eventually, Nkem had to find a new place to stay with her children. Moving out was complicated, as Chris had made modifications to the house, including closing off parts of the living room. Nkem had to carefully remove a large freezer, causing tension between her and Chris. She moved to a new accommodation after securing a job and enrolling her children in school, while awaiting the approval of her visa to return to Europe.

Nkem gets into Healthcare

As she was in a new country, she had bought some items to sell in Europe to make extra money and support her family. She had purchased Ankara fabrics, clothes, and jewelleries, which she started selling upon arrival.

One close family friend bought some of these items but never paid for them. Despite their close relationship, this woman refused to settle the debt, saying she would use the money to offset a debt her husband owed her. Nkem was taken aback and asked Eme about it, but he told her not to worry, which was another challenging experience for her.

Determined to find a stable job, Nkem first took a retail position. However, the hours were not family-friendly, so she decided to switch to healthcare. Eme was opposed to this choice, particularly disliking the idea of working with elderly people and the nature of care involved. Despite his reservations, Nkem proceeded with the training.

Upon completing her training, she was placed at a nursing home close to her home. She performed well and was soon called in for shifts when staff were sick or absent. This led to a permanent job in a care facility, and she discovered she truly enjoyed her work. She found satisfaction in talking to elderly people, listening to their stories, and making their lives easier. Their appreciation and blessings made her feel proud and valued, which encouraged her to continue in this fulfilling career.

Buying A Car

As life started improving, Nkem took on more responsibilities to support her family. She worked hard, contributing to the household and ensuring her children were well taken care of. At a certain point, she decided to take a loan from the bank to buy a car. This car wasn't for luxury, but a necessity. The family already had a car, but Eme needed it for his job, leaving her struggling to commute, especially since she often worked antisocial hours by leaving home in the evening and returning in the morning.

Having the car made her life a bit easier. She could now drive herself to work and still be back in time to take the children to school before getting some rest. Life was becoming more manageable, but Nkem's mind was full of bigger plans for the future. She dreamed of improving their lives even further and was always thinking ahead.

However, when she shared these dreams with Eme, she often felt shut down. She had big ideas–like returning to university to further her education and secure a better future for the family–but he didn't share her enthusiasm. He questioned why she was always talking about school, dismissing her ambitions as unnecessary. He seemed content with the present, having secured a decent job and holding a European passport, but Nkem was looking five, ten years ahead.

Nkem didn't give up on her dreams easily, despite Eme's lack of support. Eventually, however, feeling disheartened by his constant dismissals, she decided to stop talking about school and put her plans on hold. The weight of her unfulfilled dreams was heavy, but she kept going, focusing on her immediate responsibilities.

She continued to balance her responsibilities while pursuing her studies. Juggling a business course with caring for young children and managing a pregnancy was a challenge. Yet, she persevered, determined to finish her course. After completing her studies, she took time off to care for her newborn before returning to work. Although she did not find the ideal job, she managed to secure a part-time position, with her salary going directly towards childcare expenses.

To make extra money, Nkem began a side business called 'Nkem Snacks', making pastries and party food, which she supplied to local African shops and prepared for events with her family and prayer partner, sister Nneka. Despite the hard work, she found satisfaction in being productive. However, a family member's advice made her reconsider. This relative, who had come from Africa for a conference, accompanied her to the bakery and warned that her constant struggle and the physical demands of the business were taking a serious toll on her health. Nkem argued that she needed to make the best out of her situation, but she eventually decided to stop the pastry business. She soon relocated to another European Country.

Lessons From The Journey

Nkem sat by the window; her eyes lost in the distance as she reflected on the early days of her marriage. The warm breeze carried the scent of blooming flowers, but her thoughts were far from the peace of the present. She recalled the day she and Eme had said "yes" to each other. It was a day filled with promise, a day when they believed that love alone would carry them through the challenges ahead. But as she thought back, she realised that their journey together had been marked by missed conversations, unspoken expectations, and assumptions that had quietly shaped their lives.

From the start, both parties had entered their marriage with the hope of happiness, but neither had paused to consider what that happiness truly meant. They hadn't sat down to set boundaries, to discuss their dreams, or to plan for their future. Instead, they had fallen into the rhythm of daily life, believing that the rest would simply work itself out. But as the years passed, Nkem began to see that this approach had left gaps which were now too wide to ignore.

In those early days, she had believed that marriage was about fulfilling certain roles. She had taken pride in cooking meals, serving her husband, and creating a home where Eme could find comfort after a long day's work. He, too, had found contentment in this routine. He would come home to a warm meal, a clean house, and a wife who was always ready to meet his needs. But neither of them had questioned how long this would be enough or what would happen when the simplicity of those routines began to feel stifling.

As time went on, Nkem started to feel a growing sense of unease. The routine that had once seemed comforting now felt like a trap. She realised that their marriage had become a cycle of cooking, cleaning, and serving, with little room for dreams, growth, or meaningful connection. Eme, too, had settled into his role, but neither of them had asked the important questions: What do we want for ourselves in the next two years? Five years? Ten years? How do we want our family to grow? What are our individual responsibilities, and how do we support each other in fulfilling them?

Nkem's thoughts turned to the issue of communication. It had always been a struggle for them, hindered by a gap in age and the unspoken belief that he, as the older and supposedly wiser partner, should lead the way. She had often felt small, her voice lost in the shadow of his authority. This imbalance had made it difficult to truly connect, to share their fears, hopes, and plans for the future.

It was clear to her now that marriage needed more than love and routine to thrive. It needed communication, planning, and a shared vision for the future. Without these, even the strongest love could wither under the weight of unfulfilled expectations and unspoken needs. And as she stared out at the world beyond, she knew that the time had come to face these truths, to acknowledge the past, and to find a way forward.

Nkem sat quietly, her thoughts swirling like leaves caught in the wind. The words from the Bible in Hosea 4:6

rang in her mind: "My people are destroyed for lack of knowledge." How true those words felt now. As she reflected on her marriage to Eme, she couldn't help but think of all the things they hadn't known, all the conversations they hadn't had, and how those gaps in understanding had shaped their journey together.

He had been living in Europe, while she was in Africa. These were two very different worlds, and yet they had decided to bridge that gap and build a life together. Nkem had assumed that once married, they would live in Europe, where Eme resided. It seemed natural to her that as his wife, she would move to be with him. She never even thought to ask Eme where they would live after the wedding. It just seemed obvious that they would be together in Europe.

But looking back, Nkem wished they had discussed it. It wasn't that she minded moving to Europe; she had been excited about the idea. But now she saw that making assumptions, instead of having clear, open conversations, had been a mistake.

Eme had made many promises before they got married, but once they were together, it became clear that life wasn't going to unfold as easily as he had made it seem. Of course, he knew that life could be unpredictable, that circumstances could change, and that people could adapt. But there were things that he could have controlled, choices he could have made differently, and conversations they should have had with his wife.

Nkem thought about how Eme, as the head of their family, should have been more open with her. He should have explained his plans, his worries, and his dreams. They should have talked about their future, about where they would live, how they would handle the challenges ahead, and how they would support each other. Instead, she found herself in a marriage where so much was left unsaid, where she felt more like an observer than a partner.

Secrecy in a marriage is never beneficial. Many things went wrong for Eme, for example when he got involved in a business venture with a group of scammers. This was one of the early issues in their marriage, as he chose not to be open with Nkem about it. Instead of discussing it with her directly, she overheard him speaking about it on the phone with his family and friends. This lack of transparency created a strain, as Nkem felt excluded from important matters in their relationship.

As they began their life together, she realised that the man she had married wasn't quite the man she had envisioned. He was still the person she loved, but he was also someone who had made promises he couldn't keep. He had led her to believe that their life together would be one way, but the reality was different. And now, as she looked back on those early days, she understood that this lack of knowledge, this failure to truly communicate and plan together, had been their downfall. She learned that marriage requires effort from both partners. It's not enough for just one person to work hard; both must contribute to making the relationship work. This realisation was crucial for her. She understood that while she could control her own actions and responses, she couldn't control everything in her marriage. The experience of marriage was filled with challenges and demands that seemed endless.

Nkem's faith in God played a significant role in her journey. She firmly believed that with God by her side, she could navigate the difficulties and find strength. True strength came from within, from being mentally and emotionally prepared to handle whatever life threw at her.

Nkem sighed, feeling the weight of all the things they had missed. She knew now that marriage was about more than just love; it required knowledge, understanding, and a willingness to face the future together. As Nkem sat there, she resolved to learn from any mistakes, to seek the knowledge they had once lacked, and to find a way to rebuild what had been lost.

CHAPTER 4

Greener Pastures

U nderstanding the journey to realising and actualising your purpose and vision in life often involves
recognising the need to seek out greener pastures. Nkem
understood this early on in her life; she was certain that her
greener pastures, her "land of milk and honey," were not
back home in the country of her birth. Instead, she felt
strongly that her future lay in another land abroad. This
conviction guided her decisions and actions, reminding us
of the importance of following God's leading as we strive
to become the best versions of ourselves.

Sometimes, this journey involves leaving the familiar, stepping out of your comfort zone, and moving to a place that holds new opportunities. The Bible illustrates this with the story of Abraham in Genesis 12, where God instructs him to leave his father's land and go to a place He would show him. Like Abraham, when God gives you a dream or a vision, you might not see the full picture straight away. This is where faith plays a crucial role, keeping you on the path and moving towards the fulfilment of that vision.

Nkem confronted Eme about their future. She suggested they move to a new country to start afresh, but he changed their plans without consulting her, relocating instead, to support his brother's wife, who was having a baby. Nkem was devastated; she felt betrayed, as this was not the plan they had agreed on. When she expressed her frustration, he dismissed her concerns, insisting that the new location would be a better place to raise their children. Reluctantly, she followed him.

They lived in this land for over a decade, enduring

struggles and hardships, yet God increased them both numerically and in other ways. Nkem felt it was time to move to their own "Goshen," the land the Lord had promised them. When her passport arrived, Nkem felt it was time to make a significant change. She explained to her husband that she wanted to relocate with the children, but he was not keen on the idea. He was content with his job, but Nkem believed their life could improve if they sought new opportunities. After some negotiation, they agreed that Nkem and the children would move, while Eme would stay behind, visiting when possible.

The move was challenging. Finding a house and adjusting to a new system took time, but slowly, things began to fall into place.

Nkem focused on planning for their future, setting ambitious goals and praying for success in her new land. She wanted to be a part of her children's upbringing, so she avoided commuting to distant jobs and concentrated on local opportunities. Her interest in healthcare grew, leading her to enrol in a diploma course in health and social care, and eventually to study adult nursing at the university. Eme later joined her.

During her studies, she faced a setback when she lost her mother and had to return to Africa for the funeral. The emotional toll affected her studies, but she continued with counselling and eventually changed campuses to be closer to home.

One day, she had to attend an important training session at a church in London. A friend from another European country accompanied her there. On their way back, Eme was involved in a serious accident. Thankfully, neither Eme nor her friend was hurt, though the car was a write-off. Despite the close call, Eme was now without a vehicle, which complicated things further.

Nkem suggested renting a car to keep the business running while they waited on the insurance. Eme, however, was depressed and disheartened. His mood worsened as weeks turned into months, and he remained at home, unmotivated and unproductive. This state of affairs took a toll on the family, especially the children, who wondered why their father was always so down, spending most of his time lying on the sofa.

Despite her own struggles and the challenges of starting over in a new country, Nkem was determined to create a better life. She focused on her studies and personal growth, trying to leave past difficulties behind. When the insurance finally paid out, the amount was much less than what Eme had hoped for, and he had to look for ways to continue his business.

Unfortunately, he was soon involved in another accident, this time with a rented car. Everything seemed to be going wrong for him. Nkem continued to support him, but he remained unresponsive and dismissive of her concerns.

As they neared the end of that year, Nkem emphasised the need to settle down. They had moved across multiple countries in Europe and now, she believed, was the time to establish a permanent home. She proposed saving funds towards buying a house. Eme agreed to contribute, but his commitment was inconsistent. Nkem kept saving and pushing for their goal.

Around the same time, they were preparing for their daughter's wedding. Despite the ongoing house search and issues with unreliable agents, they eventually found a property. With Nkem's strong credit score and financial stability, she took on most of the responsibility for securing the mortgage. Despite numerous challenges, including last-minute financial demands and the support of generous friends, they managed to purchase the house. Nkem had to pause her studies to focus on work and help cover mortgage payments, unaware that a pandemic loomed on the horizon.

Eme, despite getting a new car for his business, seemed to make little progress. Nkem couldn't help but notice that the car wasn't suitable for the kind of work he did, but she chose not to argue. Their relationship was already strained, and she thought it best not to start a fight.

The pandemic brought additional complications.

Nkem had to switch to a permanent job to ensure a steady income for the mortgage and other expenses.

While she and their three adult children were working through the crisis, Eme chose to stay at home. He expressed fear about going out and dealing with the pandemic, even though others in similar situations continued working, although with reduced income. Without any savings or plans in place, Eme had not considered how to provide for his family when the pandemic hit.

One day, while Nkem was resting after a long shift, she overheard Eme talking to a friend on the phone. The friend asked how he was coping with the pandemic, and Eme admitted he was too scared to go out. This frustrated Nkem because she and her family were risking their health to work. She was doing her best to provide for the household, while Eme seemed reluctant to contribute.

Nkem's frustration grew when Eme started demanding money from her for his affairs and bills such as road tax and insurance. He wanted her to cover utility bills and other expenses, insisting it was necessary for his newly found business. Nkem, however, firmly refused. She was adamant that their home was not something to be gambled with, especially after all they had worked to achieve. She would not allow him to jeopardise their home by taking needless risks.

Despite Eme's complaints, Nkem stuck to her decision. She knew little of the business Eme was involved in and noticed that he often changed his mobile number, which only added to her confusion. The pandemic dragged on, and by the end of the year, Nkem still couldn't see any real progress from Eme.

Eventually, Eme found a new opportunity when he met a man with a business. He worked with this man for two months, earning some money. To celebrate, Eme decided to hold a barbecue, even though so many people had died during the pandemic. Nkem, exhausted from working long shifts, had to prepare for the event. On the day of the barbecue, she looked tired and stressed in the photos, while Eme seemed to enjoy the occasion.

Failed Test

Eme had been working at the same company for some time, but he felt it was time for a change. He had set his sights on a new job with the local council, specifically in the transport sector. The opportunity seemed promising, and he eagerly began making arrangements for the required driving test. On the day of the test, Eme used Nkem's car, as his vehicle wasn't available. He dropped her off at work and headed off to take the test.

Upon arriving at the test centre, the inspectors took one look at the car and flagged a major issue – all four tyres were inadequate for the test. The test was cancelled, and Eme returned home and broke the news later, as Nkem was at work.

"The tyres on your car didn't pass the test," he told her.

Nkem simply responded, "Oh, okay," expecting Eme to sort out the problem by replacing the tyres.

However, instead of discussing it further or arranging

for new tyres, Eme quietly rented a car. He booked another test, but as fate would have it, he failed again.

A few days later, during a casual conversation, Eme revealed what had happened.

"I wanted to surprise you," he said. "I went and redid the test last week, but unfortunately, I failed again. I rented a 23-plate car this time."

Nkem was stunned. "Wait, you mean to say you went and rented a car to do the test, instead of just replacing the tyres on my car like the inspectors said?"

Eme seemed unsure how to respond, and Nkem's frustration grew. "Instead of fixing the problem with the tyres, you thought, 'Why should I buy new tyres for her car?' You rented a car just to pass the test, and you still didn't pass!"

The whole situation left Nkem exasperated. It wasn't just about the tyres or the test; it was about Eme's pattern of behaviour. She felt he was always acting selfishly, as though they were in a competition rather than working together.

"If the inspectors said the tyres weren't good, why didn't you just replace them and take the same car for the test?" Nkem continued. "By doing the right thing, God would've blessed you. But instead, you went behind my back, rented a car, and still didn't pass. Now you come to me, expecting me to feel sorry for you?"

She couldn't help but feel that anyone in her position would look at Eme and wonder what he was truly up to. To her, it seemed that he was more focused on denying her any benefit than on solving the problem at hand.

Nkem was reminded of 1 Peter 3:7: "Husbands, likewise, dwell with them with understanding, giving honour to the wife, as to the weaker vessel, and as being heirs together of the grace of life, that your prayers may not be hindered." This verse calls for husbands to treat their wives with understanding and respect, valuing them as equal partners in life.

In Nkem's situation, Eme's actions highlighted a lack of communication and mutual respect. Instead of addressing the issue with the tyres by discussing it with her and taking a straightforward approach, he chose to act independently, which led to tension and mistrust. The verse reminded Nkem that a marriage should be built on understanding, honour, and unity, where both partners work together and value each other's input to maintain a harmonious relationship.

Through all these challenges, Nkem grew stronger. Her marriage had tested her resilience, teaching her to stand up for herself. Initially, she struggled to assert herself, but over time, she began to voice her concerns more firmly. This shift led to more tension with Eme, who often belittled her. He would call her names and dismiss her opinions, which hurt her deeply.

Nkem tried to remind herself that, despite his harsh words, she was doing many things right. Though she felt her efforts often went unnoticed, she knew she contributed in significant ways. She remained steadfast in her belief that she was not as foolish as he suggested, even if their marriage was far from perfect.

In the end, Nkem's determination to protect their home and stand up for herself became central to her journey. Her strength and resilience in the face of adversity became a cornerstone of her character, shaping the way she faced the ongoing challenges in her life.

Lessons from Nkem

Nkem's story is a testimony to this truth. Even when her path took an unexpected diversion to another country, she never lost sight of the vision God had given her. Her ultimate destination was the place she called the land of milk and honey. The Bible reassures us that, "He makes me to lie down in green pastures; He leads me beside the still waters." (Psalm 23:2)

It is His will for us to find ourselves in a place of abundance and peace.

In life, if you find that your efforts in one place aren't yielding results, it might be time to consider relocating. Seek God's guidance on where you should go, whether it is a different state, a different town, or even a different country. Relocating can provide a fresh start, placing you in a new environment with new opportunities. Neither age nor past challenges are barriers to starting afresh.

There is an old saying: "The grass always looks greener on the other side." While this can hold some truth, it's important to remember that even in a new land, success doesn't come automatically. It requires faith in God, hard work, integrity, and consistency. Many have gone to foreign lands and failed, not because the land wasn't full of promise, but because they did not put in the necessary effort. Wherever you find yourself, commit to doing the work, and that place will flourish for you.

CHAPTER 5

Childbearing

Nkem sat quietly on the sofa, her hands gently resting on her baby bump as she reflected on the incredible journey she had embarked upon. Childbearing had always been something she looked forward to, yet nothing could have fully prepared her for the reality of it. Even before her first child was conceived, Nkem had been diligent in her prayers. Every night, she prayed fervently for her future children, naming them in her heart long before they were born.

She and her husband, Eme, had spent countless hours discussing names, each wanting to ensure their children bore names rich in meaning and heritage. For her, choosing native names was deeply important. Growing up, she had struggled with her own name, feeling disconnected from it at times. But one day, a powerful sermon she once heard changed her perspective. The preacher had spoken about Jabez, a man whose name meant sorrow, yet whose prayer to God transformed his life. The story resonated with Nkem, and she chose to keep her name, trusting that God would shape her destiny just as He had done for Jabez.

When Nkem joined Eme in the Western world, the couple was excited to begin their life together. She still remembered that cold December when she arrived, full of hope and dreams. Just a few months later, in February, their best man and his wife welcomed a baby girl. Nkem's sister-in-law called Eme with the news, teasing him about when they would have their own child. Eme, always calm and confident, reassured her that everything would happen in God's perfect timing.

As the months passed, Nkem found herself pregnant with their first child. It was a time filled with anticipation, but also a time that revealed new challenges in her marriage. Pregnancy revealed aspects of her life she hadn't fully anticipated. While the physical changes were expected, the emotional and relational shifts were something she hadn't been prepared for. As Eme had portrayed himself as a mini-god who could not be questioned, she was left with no choice but to develop coping mechanisms to manage what had befallen her.

Through it all, Nkem's faith remained her anchor. She believed that every experience, every challenge, was shaping her into the woman and mother God intended her to be. She knew that God was with her, guiding her every step, and she trusted in His plan for her family.

The first time she held her newborn in her arms, Nkem felt a surge of gratitude and love that she could hardly describe. This tiny life, so perfect and innocent, was a testament to God's faithfulness. As she looked into her baby's eyes, Nkem knew that all the prayers, all the worries, and all the hopes she had carried in her heart had been answered in the most beautiful way.

Childbearing, for Nkem, was not just about bringing children into the world; it was about the journey of becoming a mother including learning, growing, and trusting God through each step. She felt blessed beyond measure, not just for the children she had, but for the lessons she was learning along the way. These experiences were moulding her, making her stronger, and deepening her faith in ways she never imagined.

Nkem and Eme had always believed in the importance of names. To them, names were not just labels; they were a connection to their heritage and a reflection of their faith. When it came to naming their children, they reached an agreement that felt right for both of them. Nkem, deeply connected to her roots, chose the native names, while Eme, with his strong Christian faith, selected the English names, often referred to as "Christian names." Together, they crafted names for their future children that honoured both their culture and their beliefs.

Nkem was proud of the names they had chosen. She often reflected on how these names carried the essence of their family's history and their hopes for their children's future. Each name held deep significance, and she was grateful that her children grew to love them as well. They had no complaints, and she felt a deep sense of satisfaction, knowing that each name had been carefully thought out and chosen with love.

But pregnancy brought a new set of challenges that Nkem hadn't fully anticipated. When she was pregnant with their first child, she faced a very difficult time. The first trimester was particularly hard, with severe symptoms that left her feeling weak and unable to do much. The world around her seemed to shift as she realised that what she had seen on television or heard from others about pregnancy didn't quite match her reality. Life had its own way of revealing itself, and Nkem found herself navigating through it with newfound strength.

One of the biggest surprises was how sensitive she became to certain smells and foods. The tomato stew, a staple in her home country, suddenly became unbearable for her. The mere smell of it made her nauseous, something that was particularly difficult since tomato stew was a regular meal in their household. This sensitivity made it challenging for her to cook, and it was during this time that she saw a different side of Eme.

Eme, who had always been supportive, now struggled to understand. Some days, he would come home expecting the familiar smell of tomato stew, only to find that she hadn't been able to prepare it. His reaction was not what she had hoped for; instead of empathy, she was met with frustration. It was a difficult period, and Nkem felt a growing sense of isolation.

As her pregnancy progressed and the due date approached, Eme showed his support in other ways. He accompanied her to the labour ward, staying by her side as they prepared to welcome their first child into the world. But when their baby was born, a new set of challenges emerged. Nkem had hoped for more help and understanding from Eme, but he seemed preoccupied with other things. He would go out, returning with just a packet of juice, while she lay in bed, hungry and exhausted. The physical and emotional care she needed was lacking, leaving her feeling deeply let down.

It was the support from their church community that made the difference during those early days. Nkem vividly remembered when Mama Susie, a kind woman from their church, came to stay with them. Mama Susie was a Godsend, taking care of her and the baby when she was busy. She cooked, cleaned, and even helped bathe her newborn. Nkem was deeply touched by her kindness, especially because she was struggling with a hip dislocation and a severe infection that made it impossible for her to move freely.

Other members of the church also came to help, bringing food and offering their support. One older man from their tribe even cooked yam pepper soup for Nkem, a traditional dish meant to nourish a woman after childbirth. It was during these moments that she realised just how important community was in her journey through motherhood.

As time went on, the couple faced newer challenges. When it was time to register their baby's name, they encountered unexpected complications. They had to decide on the baby's full name, including both their surnames, as Eme was not using his family name at the time, and Nkem was still using her father's name. This brought about confusion and concerns, especially when official documents started arriving with names that didn't quite align with what they had intended. It was a worry that weighed on Nkem's mind, yet she kept her faith strong, trusting that things would work out in the end.

Despite the difficulties, Nkem remained steadfast in her faith. She prayed constantly, using scripture to guide her. Proverbs 22:6 became a cornerstone of her prayers, reminding her to "train up a child in the way they should go, and when they grow old, they will not depart from it." She was determined to raise her children with a strong foundation in faith, teaching them right from wrong and being transparent with them about the realities of life.

Nkem knew that God had blessed her with these

children and that they were a heritage from the Lord. She found comfort in Psalm 127:3-5, which spoke of children as a reward from God, like arrows in the hands of a warrior. She trusted that God would not allow her to be put to shame and that her children would grow up to be strong, righteous individuals.

Through all the ups and downs, Nkem held onto her faith, believing that everything would work out for good for those who love God. She continued to pray, not just for herself but for others who were waiting on God for the fruit of the womb. She understood that the journey of motherhood was full of challenges, but she also knew that God was with her every step of the way, guiding her and giving her the strength she needed to raise her children.

At one point, Nkem considered taking on more responsibilities to support her husband, Eme. She thought about pursuing a new career but decided against it, knowing that her children needed her full attention. Instead, she found a way to balance work and family life by taking on a night job. This allowed her to be present for her children during the day, taking them to school and ensuring they were well cared for.

For over two decades, Nkem maintained this demanding routine. She worked nights and managed her home during the day, ensuring her children were never neglected. Even though the schedule was tough, she found a way to make it work without any major issues. She was grateful that her efforts allowed her to be both a provider and a present mother.

However, Nkem was always eager to learn and grow. She had a passion for nursing and wanted to pursue it at university. She discussed this with Eme, explaining that the nursing program would require her to attend classes during the day, which would mean she needed his support with the children. But Eme was hesitant; he enjoyed his routine of going to work in the morning and coming home in the evening to relax, watch football, and catch up on the news. He wasn't ready to make changes that might disrupt his comfortable life.

Nkem: "Eme, I've been thinking about something important. I really want to go to university and study nursing."

Eme: "Nursing? But how would that work? Who's going to look after the children while you're away during the day? I have my routine, you know. I work all day and when I come home, I just want to relax, watch football, and catch up on the news."

Nkem: "I understand, and I don't want to disrupt your routine. But this nursing course is something I'm passionate about. I believe it would benefit us all in the long run. What if we found someone to help with the children during the day? You could still keep your routine, and I'll be able to study."

Eme: "I don't know, Nkem. Everything's working well as it is. I'm comfortable with how things are now."

Nkem: "I know it might seem like a big change, but planning for the future is important. If I get this qualification, I could help support the family. It's not just for me, it's for all of us. Failing to plan is planning to fail."

Eme: "Hmm, I'll have to think about it. But I'm still not sure."

Nkem felt frustrated that her husband could not see the bigger picture. She believed that planning for the future was important and that change was necessary for growth. She worried that staying in the same place, both literally and figuratively, would lead to stagnation. She tried to convince him that her nursing career would benefit the whole family, but he remained firm in his decision. The Bible taught her to be submissive to her husband, so she accepted his decision, even though it wasn't what she wanted.

Nkem then suggested bringing in someone to help with the children while she pursued her studies. Eme agreed to this plan, and they invited one of Nkem's sisters to come from back home to help them look after the children. However, her sister didn't enjoy the arrangement and decided to return home. With no other options, Nkem continued to juggle her responsibilities as she had been doing, focusing on raising her children and making the best of her situation.

Despite the challenges, Nkem cherished the time she spent with her children, sharing many special moments together like Bible studies, trips to the park, and visits to reading clubs during the holidays. She was determined to ensure her children never felt neglected or unloved. She was always there for them, and they grew up knowing they could rely on their mother for anything. Psalm 127:4 says: "Like arrows in the hand of a warrior, so are the children of one's youth."

Throughout this time, Nkem kept her faith strong. She believed that God was with her every step of the way, guiding her as she raised her children. She prayed for her family constantly, asking God to bless them and keep them on the right path.

Nkem also practised the biblical principle from Habakkuk 2:2, "Write the vision and make it plain on tablets, that he may run who reads it." She would write down her prayer points, each one carefully noted and prayed over with un-wavering faith. This practice of documenting her prayers was not just a ritual, but a tangible expression of her trust in God's promises. Over time, she witnessed the remarkable faithfulness of God as each one of those prayers was answered.

This method of writing and praying over her visions became a cornerstone of her spiritual life, reinforcing her belief that when you trust in God and make your requests known to Him, He indeed answers in His perfect time.

Eventually, Nkem and her family left their home country and moved to the country of promise. For her, this move was a fulfilment of a promise she believed God had made to her. She saw this European country as a land of opportunity and blessing, a place where her family could thrive. She prayed that God would guide her to a place where she could be fulfilled and surrounded by people who would support her growth.

In Goshen, as she profoundly called the land where she

and her family inhabits, Nkem and her children became even more active members of their church as they had always served in the vineyard. They served in various ministries, including evangelism and the children's choir. Nkem felt proud of her children's involvement in the church, seeing it as an answer to her prayers. She had always wanted her children to be deeply connected to their faith, and she was grateful that they were growing up with a strong foundation in God.

After Eme joined his family, he wanted to change the routine they had established by adjusting how the family operated, but Nkem and the children resisted some of these changes. They had already established a routine and way of life that worked well for them, and they were unwilling to compromise on important things. Family prayer meetings and fasting days, for instance, were significant to Nkem and the children, who always looked forward to them. However, by the time prayer meetings arrived, the atmosphere often became tense, with the children unhappy and reluctant to participate.

Eme struggled to understand that the Bible cautions parents not to provoke their children, as it says in Ephesians 6:4: "And you, fathers, do not provoke your children to wrath, but bring them up in the training and admonition of the Lord." Unfortunately, the father's behaviour would often lead to quarrels or upsetting the children, creating tension in the house and resulting in an unhappy atmosphere.

Despite these challenges, Nkem's children remained well-adjusted and grounded. They were able to fit in wherever they went, whether it was back home in their country or in the new country. She was proud of their adaptability, how they respected others, and how they carried themselves with humility. She believed that these were the true marks of being children of God like being open to learning, meeting new people, and embracing life with kindness and grace.

Adjusting To Life With Eme

When Eme moved to the land of Goshen to join Nkem and the children, she quickly noticed something strange. Eme had a habit that seemed both odd and selfish. Whenever he went shopping for toiletries or household items, his choices were puzzling. For example, he would head to the supermarket, browse the aisles, and when it came time to choose something as simple as shower gel, he would pick the expensive brand meant specifically for men – just for himself. But for Nkem and the children, he would choose the cheapest option available.

He would bring these items home, placing his high-end shower gel in the bathroom they all shared, while leaving the cheaper one for Nkem and the kids. Naturally, being children, they would sometimes reach for Eme's shower gel instead, preferring the nicer option. Every time Eme noticed his soap was running out faster than expected, he would become frustrated, loudly complaining that no one else should use his toiletries.

One day, Nkem decided to ask him about it. "Why do you always buy the better brand for yourself, but the cheaper one for the children and me? What's the meaning of that?"

Eme seemed unfazed. "What's wrong with that?" he replied.

Nkem was baffled. "Why not buy the same brand for all of us to use?" she questioned, struggling to understand his logic.

This wasn't the only behaviour that troubled her. When Eme went to the supermarket, he would buy certain foods and items, but strictly claim them for himself, telling everyone, "Don't touch this – it's mine." Over time, the children began to follow his lead, respecting his boundaries even though the household was meant to be shared.

It wasn't just about the shower gel or the food in the fridge – it was about Eme's mindset. Nkem couldn't help but find these actions peculiar, noticing how they pointed to a deeper issue of selfishness. His constant need to keep things for himself, rather than share them with his family, was difficult to overlook and left her wondering what was truly going on in his mind.

Lessons from Marriage

As Nkem reflected on her journey, she recognised the lessons she had learned throughout her time raising her children. It hadn't been easy. Many of her colleagues at work were advancing their careers by going to university for nursing or dentistry or pursuing other courses. She chose to focus on her role as a mother. She knew that her time for career growth would come, but for now, her children were her priority. She cherished every moment of motherhood, seeing it as her calling and something deeply rewarding.

Nkem wanted her experiences to inspire others who might read her story. She knew that raising children came with challenges, but she believed that, with faith and dedication, these challenges could be overcome. Her approach was to raise her children in a godly manner, teaching them right from wrong, and being actively involved in their lives.

She was determined not to be an absentee mother. Nkem wanted to be close to her children, hoping they would feel comfortable talking to her, without fear of judgement.

One of the things Nkem cherished most was the open relationship she had with her children. They felt comfortable coming to her with their most confidential concerns and speaking to her openly. She was grateful that her children trusted her enough to share their deepest feelings, knowing she would listen without judging. When they sought her advice, she provided it with love, leaving the rest to God.

Despite her efforts, there were differences in how she and Eme approached parenting. He had his own way of doing things, shaped by his upbringing, and sometimes they didn't agree. She understood that their differing backgrounds meant they had different views on parenting. While he was often focused on his own preferences and less involved in day-to-day parenting, she worked hard to fill the gap, always present to provide the support and love her children needed.

Nkem recognised that Eme's approach, while valid from his perspective, created a distance between him and the children. He maintained a certain hierarchy and didn't always make himself approachable. She believed that being a good father involved being accessible and connected with the children, rather than just asserting authority.

Nkem thought about Proverbs 13:22: "A good man leaves an inheritance to his children's children." She understood that this inheritance wasn't just about property or money but also about character and humility. Parents need to have great character because, many times, children learn from what they see daily. Eme's behaviour showed how important it was for parents to live out the values they wanted their children to inherit.

Looking back, Nkem was thankful for the grace and strength God had given her throughout her journey as a mother. She knew that her success in raising her children and eventually becoming a grandmother was not due to her abilities alone, it was the help of God almighty.

As she wrapped up her reflections, Nkem gave thanks to God for His continuous presence in her life. She acknowledged that it was God's grace that had carried her through all the ups and downs of motherhood. She felt a deep sense of gratitude and was ready to end this chapter of her story with praise and honour to God. If there was anything more she wished to add, she knew she would return to it another day, but for now, she was content with sharing her journey and lessons learned.

CHAPTER 6

Name, Identity
and Attributes

Nkem had always been interested by the significance of names and their impact on identity. Over time, she got deep into the subject, learning that names are not just labels but carry profound meanings and attributes. Names are crucial because they define who we are, reflect our cultural backgrounds, and often indicate our heritage. They can even shape how we perceive ourselves and how others respond to us.

1 Chronicles 4:9-10 says: "Now Jabez was more honourable than his brothers, and his mother called his name Jabez, saying, "Because I bore him in pain." And Jabez called on the God of Israel, saying, "Oh, that You would bless me indeed, and enlarge my territory, that Your hand would be with me, and that You would keep me from evil, that I may not cause pain!" So God granted him what he requested."

Jabez wasn't popular but was an honourable man according to Scripture. His name meant pain and sorrow, reflecting his mother's state at the time of his birth. However, Jabez prayed to the God of Israel to change his name and situation, to bless him, enlarge his territory, and keep him from harm. And God answered him. I pray that all who are reading this book will find that the God of Israel changes every sorrow and pain in your lives, blesses you, and enlarges your territory. In Jesus' name.

In her studies, Nkem discovered that names hold power and responsibility. This concept is not only evident in everyday life but also highlighted in the Bible. In the beginning, when God created Adam and Eve, He gave them names, signifying their identities and roles. God created Adam in His own image and bestowed upon him the power and dominion to name all the creatures He had made. This act of naming demonstrated authority and responsibility, showing how important names are in establishing one's role and influence.

The Bible also illustrates the importance of names through various examples. For instance, in the book of Isaiah 43:1, it is written that God calls us by name and declares that we are His. This reinforces the idea that names are deeply significant in our relationship with God and our sense of belonging.

Nkem studied the changes in names within the Bible to understand their importance better. For example, Abraham, originally named Abram, was renamed by God to signify his new role as the father of many nations (Genesis 17:5). Similarly, Sarah's name was changed from Sarai to Sarah as part of God's promise that she would bear a son, Isaac.

Another notable example is Jacob, who was renamed Israel after his encounter with God. This change marked a transformation in his identity and destiny. The story of Naomi in the book of Ruth also illustrates the impact of names. After experiencing great sorrow, Naomi changed her name to Mara, meaning "bitter," reflecting her personal suffering. Although others continued to call her Naomi, her choice of name showed her changed perspective on life (Ruth 1:20).

These biblical examples show that names can reflect a person's journey, their relationship with God, and their role in the world. Nkem discovered that names are not merely a way to identify individuals but also carry the weight of their experiences, responsibilities, and destinies.

Through her exploration of names and their significance, she learned that names can be powerful symbols of identity and purpose. They can represent blessings, responsibilities, and the essence of a person's life journey. Understanding this, she became even more appreciative of the names she had given her own children, recognising them as a fundamental part of their identity and future.

Nkem's Name Situation

Nkem had always understood the importance of names, both as a symbol of identity and as a reflection of culture and tradition. However, her own experience with names had been far from straightforward, causing her much concern over the years. In her culture, as well as in many others, it was customary for a woman to take on her husband's surname upon marriage. This was a tradition she had expected to follow, just as it was done in the Bible, where a married woman would adopt her husband's name. But in Nkem's case, things turned out differently.

As mentioned earlier, when Nkem married Eme, she was surprised to find that he did not insist on her taking his surname. Instead, she chose to keep her family name and passed it on to their children. This decision puzzled and troubled Nkem, as it went against the norms she had grown up with. She felt that it was important for the children to bear their father's name, as was customary, and she raised the issue with Eme multiple times. Each time, he would brush off her concerns, telling her not to worry and that the right time for a name change would come.

Despite Eme's reassurances, the issue weighed heavily on Nkem's heart. As their children grew older and started school, the matter of their surname became more complicated. The children's school records listed Nkem's family name as their surname, but their birth certificates showed both parents' surnames. This led to confusion, especially when the children travelled abroad. She recalled an incident where the school booked tickets for a trip using the children's school surnames, only to discover that their passports bore a different name. The discrepancy caused a great deal of trouble, with her requiring her to write letters to airlines and deal with the administrative chaos that ensued.

The situation came to a head when Nkem herself faced awkward moments because of her name. On several occasions, people questioned her marital status, as her surname remained her maiden name. At times, when she introduced herself using her maiden name, it led to misunderstandings and even ridicule, particularly in social settings. People found it strange that she was a "Mrs" yet did not carry her husband's surname. This left her feeling embarrassed and out of place, even though she knew she was fully entitled to her own identity.

One of the most challenging moments came when Eme joined the family in their new home abroad, in what she referred to as the land of their Goshen. By then, Nkem had grown accustomed to her maiden name and had made peace with it, despite the complications it caused. However, he decided it was time to settle the name issue once and for all. He arranged for a deed poll to officially change the children's surnames to his family name and suggested that his wife should do the same.

But Nkem refused. After many years of living with her maiden name, she had grown comfortable with it. More importantly, her children's identities were tied to that name, as it was what appeared on their birth certificates and passports. Changing her surname after so many years of marriage seemed unnecessary and burdensome to her. She also didn't want to deal with the hassle of updating her name across various official documents and qualifications.

Despite the decision to change the children's names, the issue did not completely disappear. It continued to surface in various forms, particularly when dealing with legal or financial matters where the discrepancy between names caused confusion. Even in church, where Nkem sometimes used her husband's family name to avoid questions, the underlying issue remained unresolved.

The situation reached a critical point when the children, who had been born in a Western country and held European nationality from birth, were stripped of their citizenship upon becoming adults. The authorities argued that since neither parent was a national of the country and because the children's names had been changed, they were no longer entitled to their passports. This created a huge problem for the family, adding to the stress and pressure that had already plagued them for years.

But through all the difficulties, Nkem held onto her faith. She believed that God would see them through, and indeed, He did. The challenges they faced with names and identity were significant, but they managed to navigate them with perseverance and prayer.

Lessons From The Names Situation

Nkem's experience taught her valuable lessons about the importance of names and identity. She realised that the decisions parents make regarding their children's names can have lasting consequences. It was a lesson she hoped others would learn from, especially couples who might not fully consider the implications of their choices. She and Eme had used her family name for their children, but the complexities it brought into their lives showed how crucial it is to think carefully about such decisions.

Nkem reflected on the importance of doing the right thing and ensuring that one's records are always in order. She realised that if her children had lived a life that was less than upright, if they had made poor choices or engaged in questionable activities, the situation could have turned out much worse. When the authorities reviewed their records and background to issue new passports, they looked into every detail: where they had lived, what kind of life they had led, and whether their parents had been truthful about their history. It was a thorough investigation, one that could have unearthed any hidden issues.

In the end, she accepted that names, while important, are just one part of a person's identity. What mattered most was the love and unity within the family, and she remained proud of her name and the legacy it represented.

CHAPTER 7

Balancing Family, Work and Faith

Proverbs 19:21 reads: "There are many plans in a man's heart, Nevertheless the Lord's counsel that will stand."

Nkem found herself caught in the delicate balance of family, work, and faith. Her husband, Eme, had been in and out of jobs, and this instability weighed heavily on her. Each time he lost his job, it was a challenge, especially when he seemed indifferent to the situation. She noticed this pattern, and it bothered her deeply. Although she had a permanent job, she took on side jobs to support her large family and ensure they could meet their needs. She was always working, always thinking ahead, trying to keep everything in order.

Their son had a school trip abroad, which Nkem had paid for in instalments. Just before the trip, he handed their son a large sum of money without consulting her. When the boy returned, he had spent every penny on shopping, much to her dismay. She was frustrated but held her peace, knowing that the lesson had been learned, even if it was the hard way.

Their daughter, too, went on a school trip, though her destination was within their continent. She was given money as well, but she returned with some of it unspent. The contrast between their children's spending habits was stark, and she took note of it. She realised that each child was different, and so were their ways of handling responsibility.

As the children grew, Nkem had to make tough decisions. She had been supporting their extracurricular activities, like swimming and dance, but with the financial strain, she decided to cut back. However, before stopping the dance lessons, she allowed her daughter to participate in an international dance event at Disneyland. It was a memorable experience for the family, though her dad couldn't join them due to work. This had to be done as she felt it was time for her to follow her heart to actualise her dream in nursing.

Nkem continued her studies while working, saving, and praying for better days. They were also trying to buy a house, and when things didn't go as planned with the bank, she decided to take a year off from university to focus on working and securing their mortgage. It was a difficult time, but she was determined not to let her family down.

His frequent job losses continued to be a source of tension. He would be out of work for months, and she would be the first to notice. She urged him to take on multiple jobs to provide stability, but he didn't heed her advice. He had lost his licence and had to switch to a different kind of work, which was less reliable. Despite her suggestions, he chose to handle things in his own way, often leaving her to pick up the pieces.

Nkem wasn't trying to compete with Eme; she just wanted to ensure the well-being of their family. She knew that with a large family, it was crucial to have a steady income. So, she worked tirelessly, taking on extra jobs, managing the household, and praying for strength.

When Nkem moved to Goshen, Eme decided to join her and resigned from his job. He had planned to use his pension savings to buy property, but instead, he used the money to buy a car for his business. She was disheartened by this decision, particularly since the car turned out to be problematic. Eme faced frequent issues with the vehicle, but after returning it and buying another, he started his business. He did this without a formal agreement with his wife. You can imagine the potential problems that could arise within the family. He claimed it was his money and questioned why Nkem should have a say in how it was used.

Nkem observed his business struggles and tried to offer advice, but he dismissed her concerns. He frequently complained about financial difficulties and sought help from others in his field. Despite these challenges, she remained focused on her path and continued to work towards the goals she had set.

Eme's new car didn't seem to improve his situation. He appeared to be more distracted than ever, and his involvement with a transport company added to the confusion. Late at night, he would leave with a blanket and spend hours in his car, waiting for calls that rarely came. Nkem found this troubling, especially since he never explained what he was doing.

In the midst of all this, her faith remained unshaken. She believed that with God, all things were possible. She prayed for her family, for Eme to find stable work, and for their financial situation to improve. Though she knew it wasn't easy, she trusted that God would see them through the challenges they faced.

She found herself in a difficult situation, one that tested

her patience and strength every day. Eme, her husband, had grown increasingly detached from the responsibilities of their household, leaving most of the burden on her shoulders. It wasn't just the financial stress of him being in and out of jobs; it was also the absence of support in the daily tasks that wore her down.

She remembered a particular day during the pandemic when she came home, exhausted after working several long shifts. The weariness weighed on her as she entered the kitchen to prepare something to eat, only to find Eme lounging on the couch, absorbed in football and the news. This was his routine whenever he was out of work; spending mornings watching gospel preachers and praying, and the rest of the day in front of the TV. Nkem, tired and hungry, made a simple meal for herself and sat down to eat.

Eme, noticing that she had prepared food, got up and went to the kitchen, expecting to find something for himself. When he realised she hadn't cooked for him, he confronted her, accusing her of being wicked. Nkem, drained and discouraged, simply agreed. "Yes, I know," she said and continued eating. His words hurt, but she had no energy left to argue. It wasn't the first time she had seen this side of him. She had experienced his lack of empathy before, especially during the births of their children, when he had shown little understanding or care. He had even called her 'stupid' on more than one occasion in the presence of the children.

To Nkem, it seemed as though he didn't grasp the concept of caring beyond words. He could speak as if he cared, but his actions rarely followed through. She had accepted that he was a typical African man, holding onto the belief that cooking and domestic duties were solely the woman's responsibility. This mindset frustrated her, especially since she had grown up seeing her own father, a man who didn't have much education, helping her mother with cooking and other household tasks. She had hoped for a similar partnership with Eme, but it was not to be. She was not comparing them; but rather hoping for improvement. One of the books she read growing up was titled *The Beautiful Ones Are Not Yet Born*, and it left her with the belief that the new should always be better than the old. To illustrate, consider cars: newer models are generally better than their predecessors, and that's a fact.

In the early days, the only thing Eme would cook was a simple breakfast of fried plantain and eggs. But as she became more consumed by work, doing everything she could to keep the family afloat, she noticed a shift. She was working so much that even on her days off, she was too exhausted to do anything. It was only when Eme found himself hungry, with nothing prepared in the fridge, that he began to cook more regularly. Yet she knew he wasn't doing it out of love or a desire to support her; he was doing it because he had no other choice.

The food he cooked didn't matter much to her. She was too tired, too disheartened by the situation. She rarely ate the meals he made, and the children followed suit. Eme had set a standard; he used to get upset if anyone touched the food he kept in the fridge for himself, so the children had learned to avoid it. Even when she assured them it was okay to eat, they preferred to find something else.

Her frustration grew, not only because she didn't receive help, but also due to the absence of genuine care. His actions came too late, and they lacked the warmth and love that could have made a difference. Instead, Nkem felt as though she was living with a man who acted out of obligation, rather than a shared sense of responsibility or affection. The burden of maintaining their home, providing for the family, and keeping everything together weighed heavily on her, and there was little comfort in knowing that, when things got tough, she was mostly on her own.

Lessons and Reflections

During the pandemic, life changed for everyone, but for Nkem, one thing that stood out was Eme's unusual behaviour. At that time, Eme had lost his job and wasn't working. He had been using a rented car for work, but when the pandemic hit, he stopped going out. The car sat parked in the street for more than two or three months. Nkem kept telling him to return it, reminding him, "You should call the owner to come and collect the car before someone damages it, and it becomes your problem." However, it took a long time before Eme did anything, and eventually, the owner came to take the car back.

During this period, Eme spent most of his time at home. He wasn't working, and instead, he spent his days either sleeping, watching TV, or just moving around the house without doing much. Proverbs 24:33-34 says "A little sleep, a little slumber, a little folding of the hands to rest; So shall your poverty come like a prowler, and your need like an armed man."

Nkem, on the other hand, continued to go to work every day, returning home exhausted. What frustrated her the most was that Eme always talked about how much he loved her and wanted the best for their family, yet his actions never reflected his words.

One thing that especially bothered Nkem was the state of her car. For weeks, even months, she hadn't been able to get it washed, as most places were closed. Although Nkem didn't ask Eme directly to wash her car, she felt it was something any caring husband would have done, especially since he was home all day. But Eme never did.

Nkem clearly remembered the first time she washed her car during the pandemic. The car was filthy – covered in dirt from rain and dust, so much so that the number plates were barely visible. She spent the afternoon scrubbing the car in the driveway, going back and forth to get water. Eme could see her from the living room window, but he simply sat there, watching TV, not offering to help. Nkem found it strange, but she said nothing.

Another time, as the lockdown began to ease, Nkem washed her car again, preparing for a special occasion. They had been invited to a birthday celebration of a family friend at church, and Nkem wanted the car to be clean for the event. After spending the day making sure the car was spotless, she felt proud of her work. When the weekend came, and they were ready to leave for the party, Eme offered to drive.

Nkem quickly responded, "No, I'll drive. I just washed

the car two days ago, and I want to keep it clean."

So she took the driver's seat, and they made their way to the party.

Though these incidents may have seemed small, to Nkem, they highlighted a pattern in Eme's behaviour that she found strange. He could watch her struggle with simple tasks, like washing the car, but never stepped in to help. It made Nkem feel as though she was carrying the burden alone, even when they were supposed to be partners.

Nkem continued with her work, doing what she could to keep everything together despite the challenges she faced. The pandemic had forced everyone indoors, and, like many others, her family adapted to the new reality. They attended church services online, which made life a bit easier for her. Whenever she could, she joined the people of God in worship from the comfort of her home. It was a small comfort amidst the chaos.

When the pandemic restrictions were lifted, and people started returning to church, she didn't go back immediately. She was still deep in her studies, working on a project that demanded her full attention. Even when she had the time, she chose to worship from home, focusing on completing her studies. After finishing her project and handing it in, she continued with her work, pushing through each day with determination. In the end, she gave all the glory to God. Despite everything that was happening around her, she hadn't given up on her faith.

Nkem had made a promise to God, a promise that no matter what challenges or storms came her way, she and her household would serve the Lord. She held firmly to this commitment, reminding herself of the scripture from Joshua 24:15, which declared, "As for me and my house, we will serve the Lord." This verse was her anchor, her source of strength amid all her struggles. She prayed fervently, and through it all, Jehovah saw her and her family through.

The battles were constant, but she felt God's presence every step of the way. One of the Bible passages that sustained her was Psalm 121, particularly verse 1: "I will lift up my eyes to the hills, from where comes my help? My help comes from the Lord." This verse resonated deeply with her, especially when she realised that Eme was no longer there for her in the way she needed. She understood that her help could only come from God. She stopped looking to him for support and placed all her trust in the Lord.

The Bible also reminded her of the danger of relying on man, as it says, "Woe unto him who looks to man." She knew that everything she needed could only come from God, so she focused her energy and faith on Him. Nkem and her children continued to serve God in every way they could. They remained committed, and God, in His faithfulness, never let them down. She often called Him by His names, for example, Ebenezer, Jehovah Rapha, Jehovah Nissi, always acknowledging His presence and help in every aspect of her life.

God had shown His faithfulness time and time again, in her career, in her home, and in the lives of her children. Despite the challenges and the trials that seemed to follow them, Nkem never doubted God's goodness. People might wonder how she could continue to serve God in the face of so many difficulties, but she held firm in her belief that her Redeemer was alive. It didn't matter what others thought or said; only obedience to God mattered to her. The peace in her life was not the absence of problems but the presence of God.

She drew strength from the story of Jesus where He said to the accusers of the adulterous woman, "He who is without sin among you, let him throw a stone at her first" (John 8:7). When Jesus looked around, everyone had disappeared, recognising their own sinfulness. Nkem understood that everyone, including her accusers, had sinned. The enemy might try to bring her down, but she knew that God was always there, faithful in every situation.

Nkem thanked God for the strength and the ability to rise above all her circumstances. Despite the challenges that tried to weigh her down, whether in her family, her career, or her faith, God lifted her head high. He reminded her that she was chosen, and that no matter what life threw at her, He would be there to watch over her. Through it all, God remained faithful, not just to her, but also in the lives of Eme and their children.

Love, Accountability, and Repeated Mistakes

There's an important lesson to be drawn from Nkem's experience, one rooted in biblical principles of love and accountability. The Bible teaches that love does not keep a record of wrongs; it is patient, enduring, and full of grace. Nkem knew this well, but there was an instance with Eme that truly tested her understanding of these principles.

One particular day, Eme had taken Nkem's car out and parked it somewhere. A few weeks later, a parking ticket arrived in the post. Since the car was registered in Nkem's name, she was the one who received the bill. The ticket indicated that the car had been parked at a local centre for several hours, which left her confused. Checking her work rota, she confirmed she had been at work on that day, so it couldn't have been her who parked the car.

She approached Eme about the situation, asking if he had been to that location. Eme denied it, insisting that he hadn't gone to the place mentioned on the ticket. However, the dates and times on the fine didn't add up. Something wasn't right.

Nkem then asked him directly, "Did you go into a betting shop or somewhere nearby and forget you parked the car?"

What puzzled her even more wasn't just the ticket itself but Eme's casual response to the situation. It was this kind of behaviour, denial, and lack of responsibility that Nkem found troubling. As much as the Bible teaches that love endures and "love...keeps no record of wrongs" (1 Corinthians 13:5), it also teaches that one cannot continue in sin and expect grace to always abound.

At one point, Eme had been using the car to get to work and hadn't paid the tolls for about two to three weeks in a row. The bills were being sent to their old address because Nkem had forgotten to change it when they moved. After a while, she started getting messages on her phone with threatening warnings, but she thought they were scams and ignored them.

Then, one day, a large stack of letters arrived in the post – over twenty envelopes, all the same. Nkem's daughter picked them up and called her at work, saying she was scared by the number of letters in her name. Nkem told her to open one and check what it was about. To their shock, it was a threatening letter, but her daughter couldn't quite figure out who Nkem owed the money to. She reassured Nkem not to worry and that she would sort it out.

By the time Nkem got home, her daughter had figured it out. Eme had racked up nearly £3,000 in debt under Nkem's name. Each of the original fines had been £5, but because the letters had been going to the old address, the amount had built up. Nkem was devastated and sent photos of the letters to Eme, his older brother, and their family friends.

Eme immediately blamed Nkem, asking why she hadn't changed the address, and pointed out that the money was coming out of his account anyway. One of their family friends' husbands advised them to write a letter to the company and explain the situation, and that was how it was eventually resolved.

This reminded Nkem of Romans 6:23, "For the wages of sin is death, but the gift of God is eternal life in Christ Jesus our Lord." There comes a time when repeated wrongdoing has consequences, and she knew this situation with Eme was more than just about a toll or parking fine; it was a reflection of a deeper issue.

Nkem reflected on this deeply. She knew love required patience, but it also called for change, for growth, and for taking responsibility for one's actions. She believed that repeatedly making the same mistakes without learning from them wasn't just an error; it was a failure to honour the spirit of love and forgiveness.

For Nkem, this situation with Eme was not just about a parking fine – it was a reflection of a broader issue in their relationship. Love may endure all things, but it does not mean covering up wrongs without accountability. True love, as Nkem understood, required not only forgiveness but also repentance and a genuine desire to improve.

Romans 6:1-2 also rang in her mind: "Shall we continue in sin that grace may abound? Certainly not!" This scripture captured how Nkem felt – there was a point where patience and love must be met with real change. Would Eme ever take full responsibility for his actions, or would he continue to rely on her forgiveness without making any effort to change?

CHAPTER 8

Following Your Heart

Jeremiah 1:5 "Before I formed you in the womb I knew you; Before you were born I sanctified you; I ordained you a prophet to the nations." Nkem had always believed that God had a special plan for her. She held onto this promise, trusting that her life was guided by a divine purpose, even when the path ahead seemed unclear.

One memory from her childhood stood out vividly. As one of the youngest children, she often accompanied her parents to work. When she reached school age, she stopped joining them, focusing instead on her education. However, when her older sister had a baby, she was pulled out of school to help care for the child. She resented this interruption, but in her family, there was little room to question her parents' decisions.

Nkem was unhappy living with her sister, feeling as though her education was slipping away. She vividly remembered an incident that strengthened her resolve. Her sister's husband (may his soul rest in peace) had refused to send his own brother to the farm, insisting that the boy needed to attend school. She overheard this and felt a deep sense of injustice. Why was she, too, not at school? This event ignited a determination in her to return home and continue her education, no matter the cost.

One day, without telling anyone, she left her sister's house and began the long journey back to her family's home, walking along a dangerous, lonely path. When her sister's husband finally caught up with her, he tried to persuade her to return, but she refused. She wanted to go back to school, and nothing would change her mind. She was taken back to school, but by then, she had already missed a year. Her classmates had moved on, and she had to repeat the year.

The setback only made her stronger. She was determined not to let her education slip away again. After finishing primary school, she set her sights on secondary school and beyond. However, her family posed another challenge. Her father, although supportive in his own way, believed that their limited resources should be used for her brother's education rather than hers. Her mother echoed this sentiment. It wasn't due to a lack of resources; rather, her parents' perception was that a woman should not pursue higher education but should marry and start a family, while the man should receive an education to prepare himself as the future head of his own family.

She took entrance exams for both university and polytechnic, but when her results came back, she was faced with another hurdle. Although she had done well overall, she had only received passing grades in maths and English. Her grades were not high enough to qualify her for university admission. Disappointed but undeterred, she decided to visit the Polytechnic in her state to see if there was any way she could continue her education.

There, she met with the chancellor, a man from her community. After reviewing her scores and recognising her determination, he offered her a place in a remedial program. If she successfully completed the program, she would be eligible to pursue her National Diploma the following academic year.

Nkem was overjoyed. She returned home and told her father that she did not want to pursue the apprenticeship; she wanted to go to school instead. Her father, however, concerned about the financial burden, insisted that they could not afford it. He was concerned that the money they had was intended for her brother's education, not for her studies, and insisted that she should proceed with the apprenticeship. But Nkem was resolute. She knew that God had a plan for her, a plan that went beyond what her parents could see or understand. She would find a way, just as she always had.

Nkem was determined to continue her education despite the obstacles her parents had placed in her path. When her father refused to support her financially, she decided to take matters into her own hands. She began to ask extended relatives for help, seeking small amounts of money from anyone willing to assist her. It wasn't that her parents didn't have the money; her mother simply believed she should start working instead of pursuing further studies. She was focussed.

She managed to raise enough money to pay for her school fees and accommodation. When she returned home, she informed her parents that she was going back to school. They could not deter her. Nkem left and started her studies, relying on the small financial support her sister, who was working at the time, could offer. Whenever she was on holiday, Nkem engaged in petty trading, selling sweet roasted corn, pears, oranges and other items to make some extra money. She also received a state bursary, which helped her cover her expenses.

It wasn't until after her matriculation ceremony that

her parents began to see the seriousness of her ambitions. Her mother attended the event, and afterward, her father finally started to support her, giving her money for her school fees and upkeep. Though her older brother, who lived in the Western world, was of little help, Nkem remained undeterred. She had already become a born-again Christian, and her faith connected her with career-focused, like-minded people in the church.

Through her church, Nkem found a place to do her one-year industrial training at a petrochemical company. This opportunity was a turning point for her. The company paid her well and even provided transport to and from work. It was during this time that her future husband, Eme, proposed to her. After completing her industrial training, Nkem returned to school to pursue her Higher National Diploma (HND). She was determined to achieve her goals, and by the time she finished her HND, she was ready for the next step in her life.

Pursuing her HND was made easier because God turned everything around. Her parents were highly supportive, and her fiancé Eme also supported her financially, which allowed her to live in abundance. This continued until they both had their traditional and church wedding ceremonies, which were not easy decisions to make.

When Nkem married Eme, she knew she wanted to pursue a career in nursing. She had heard many stories about how well nurses in the Western world were paid, and she was determined to join their ranks. However, when she joined Eme in a non-English-speaking country, she found herself frustrated. She was determined to move to an English-speaking country to make her dream a reality. He had promised to support her education, but every time she mentioned school, it seemed to trigger something in him, making him resistant.

Before Nkem, Eme, and their children moved to an English-speaking country, there had been extensive discussions and considerations about the decision. It wasn't an easy one, but it seemed the best course of action for the entire family. The move wasn't motivated solely by her desire to pursue a nursing career; they were also living in a non-English-speaking country, where Nkem's residency permit had expired. The authorities required documents that she couldn't provide, as they weren't genuinely hers.

Nkem and Eme agreed that they would return to their home country to sort everything out. This plan would also allow her to serve her nation, keeping her occupied while they worked on processing the necessary documents. Upon their return, she enrolled the children in school and tried to adjust to the new reality.

Initially, they agreed on the next country they would move to. However, after he returned to their home country and then went back abroad, he called her with unexpected news. He informed her that they would no longer be moving to the country they had originally planned. Instead, he suggested they move to a different English-speaking country. When she asked why, Eme explained that after conducting research and speaking with other families, he believed this new country would be a better place to raise their children.

Nkem was taken aback. She pointed out that the decision was one they agreed to make as a family, not one influenced by others. She insisted that they should stick to the original plan. However, he remained adamant and chose to move to the new country. This left Nkem frustrated and disappointed. She tried to involve both her family and his in the matter, but eventually, she turned to prayer for guidance.

In her prayers, Nkem felt a clear message from God, telling her to go wherever her husband was. Although she could sense that his decisions were influenced by the fact that his status provided them with the legal standing they needed, which he may have felt gave him more control, Nkem decided to follow him. She realised that for the sake of their family, it was important to remain united.

They eventually moved to the country he had chosen. Nkem didn't like the decision, but she accepted it and prayed for strength and guidance from God.

Eventually, they moved to an English-speaking

country, but Nkem's struggles continued. She found herself doing various jobs, always striving to excel. She enrolled in different courses to improve her skills, even earning distinctions. But each time her exam results arrived, he would open the letters before she got home, and although he would congratulate her, she couldn't shake the feeling that her successes made him feel insecure.

Despite the challenges, she continued to push forward. She loved learning and was committed to finishing every course she started, no matter how difficult. However, when it came time to pursue her nursing career, she faced new obstacles. He was unwilling to help with childcare, even though she needed his support to attend school. They tried to bring her sister over to help, but she couldn't adjust to the cold climate and returned to Africa after a month. Frustrated, Nkem decided to leave it in God's hands, believing that her time would come.

Unable to pursue nursing immediately, she enrolled in a business course at university and earned an honours degree. She found a job in an NGO, but her heart wasn't in it. She longed for something more fulfilling. As her children grew, she continued to support them, ensuring they had everything they needed. Yet, she knew her fight for her dreams was far from over.

Eventually, Nkem realised that her true passion lay in healthcare. She returned to work in the healthcare sector, and her love for the field grew. Despite the many setbacks she had faced, Nkem never gave up. She had chosen to follow her heart, and through determination and faith, she had liberated herself from the limitations others had tried to impose on her.

She pursued a diploma in Health and Social Care. Alongside this, she took courses in Maths and English to strengthen her academic foundation. By the time she completed her studies, her husband Eme had joined the family, offering some support as she prepared for the next step in her journey.

Determined to achieve her dream, Nkem enrolled in university to study nursing. The journey was not easy;

having not studied pure sciences in secondary school, she found the biological sciences and physics particularly challenging. Yet, through perseverance and faith, she pressed on, balancing her studies with work and placements. All glory to God, Nkem eventually qualified as a staff nurse.

Her first job after qualifying was fulfilling, but it came with its own set of challenges. Nkem realised that she didn't want to be tied down to night shifts or working weekends, missing out on time with her family and fun activities. She prayed about it, asking God for a job that would allow her to work Monday to Friday, or perhaps Monday to Thursday, with only one Saturday shift a month. Miraculously, her prayers were answered, and she secured a job with exactly those conditions.

A woman's life doesn't end in the kitchen or in domestic duties. It's important to create a life that works for you, to follow your heart and dreams. Her parents had raised her with the belief that a woman's life revolved around the kitchen, but she had defied that expectation. She still loved cooking and being a traditional, family-oriented person, but she believed there was nothing wrong with balancing a career alongside those responsibilities.

Women should understand that contributing to the home, both financially and emotionally, makes life more meaningful and fulfilling. It's not about diminishing the importance of domestic work like cleaning, cooking, and looking after the family are significant, unpaid jobs that often go unnoticed. But women need more than that; they need to go out, have a career, meet people, and have a sense of fulfilment beyond the home.

Working outside the home also provides opportunities to share your faith, to build relationships, and to feel good about yourself. Commit to being a lifelong learner so you can become a better version of yourself. Self-care is essential to keep a healthy mind. Everyone is equal in God's eyes, but on Earth, people do measure each other, often sizing each other up based on their achievements. Study Job Chapter 1 and you will learn of Job who was a great man who feared God and had lots of blessings. He lost it all but it was for a reason.

Women should strive to be what God intended them to be, which is to be empowered, helpful to society, and a blessing to their families and communities. In the Bible, women like Deborah and Abigail made significant contributions despite the challenges they faced. Deborah was a Prophetess and Judge of Israel at a time, as described in Judges 4 and 5. Abigail, originally the wife of Nabal, later became the wife of King David, as noted in 1 Samuel 25.

Men, too, should support and allow things to work as they should, to enable both men and women to fulfil their God-given purposes. May anyone reading this story find salvation, peace, and liberation, and may your dreams be actualised.

CHAPTER 9

God as the Centrepiece

The Bible says that He knows the end from the beginning, and His thoughts are not our thoughts; He is the wise God. Nkem loved a Bible verse from Job 3:25: "For the things I greatly feared have come upon me, and what I dreaded has happened to me." Despite the challenges and fears, God showed her immense mercy throughout her journey.

Another verse that was her comfort is Isaiah 46:10 which reads: "Declaring the end from the beginning, and from ancient times things that are not yet done, saying, 'My counsel shall stand, and I will do all My pleasure.'"

Nkem was deeply family-oriented and valued both her nuclear and extended family. She would do anything for them. However, there came a time when she decided to focus more on her immediate family, especially as her children grew up. When they were younger, she had no problem putting all the children in one room to accommodate visitors, like uncles and aunties who came to visit while on holidays. She would cook, serve everyone, and manage all the expenses, and the children enjoyed the company.

But as the children grew older, Nkem felt it was time for a change. She suggested that visitors start staying in hotels or Airbnbs rather than at their homes, which reduced the frequency of how they entertained extended family members. This idea, however, was met with resistance from Eme, who did not agree with the change.

Nkem had become an even more prayerful person, and she maintained her spiritual practices diligently. At one point, her husband complained that her morning prayers disturbed him, and he even began using her prayer points against her during conflicts. In response, she adapted by finding quieter times for prayer, such as walking in the park on her days off, and continued her daily Bible readings and spiritual meditation. Despite these challenges, she felt assured that God's plan for her life and her family was unfolding as intended.

At some point, Eme turned to online businesses and network marketing. He asked her to change all the utility bills to his new network provider to get discounts. She refused, saying she did not want to risk their property and well-being for an online scheme. He was furious, but she stood her ground. Though he managed to switch some services and get a commission, the service quality was poor, and he eventually reverted to his previous provider.

Through all these struggles, Nkem remained steadfast, knowing that God's plan for them was greater than their current challenges. Despite difficulties and setbacks, God's masterpiece is always at work, guiding and shaping their lives according to His perfect plan.

God helped her despite all the pain she had endured. She has worked tirelessly to support her husband and take on family responsibilities. Even when he was unable to contribute, she always stepped in to fill the gaps. Yet his insecurities led him to express dissatisfaction with the support she provided. He told their children that the money Nkem spent was "our money" and that every expense should be carefully considered, focusing on family needs rather than unnecessary things.

Loss of Power

Shortly after Eme travelled to a different country for work, Nkem found herself in a difficult situation back in the non-English-speaking country where they lived. Eme had gone to secure a job with the plan of eventually sorting out Nkem's documents so she could return home and legalise her stay. Meanwhile, Nkem was left alone, seven months pregnant, with their young son still in the buggy, trying to manage life in a foreign land.

Eme also failed to teach his wife how to use the ATM

when they first moved abroad, leaving her in the dark about managing finances for a long time. They lived together for about two years before Nkem had to learn how to use the ATM when he went to work in a different country. This lack of basic financial education was a serious oversight on his part, highlighting how he took advantage of his wife's naivety.

Nkem had always respected his authority and decisions, believing that, as the older partner, he should make all major decisions. She had embraced this role, hoping to be a dutiful wife, but she did not anticipate that circumstances would change.

Eme, being ten years older than Nkem, assumed that his age and experience gave him sole authority in decision-making. This power imbalance meant that her opinions or contributions were often disregarded. Yet, Nkem continued to support and uplift her family, even as Eme's attitude became increasingly unreasonable.

To every young girl, woman, and widow, I encourage

you to learn from this life story and place your trust in God. The Bible tells us that God is the "Author and Finisher of our faith," and for the joy set before Him, He endured great suffering. Her message is to remind others that despite challenges, relying on God and working diligently is essential. As Proverbs 10:4 says, "Laziness leads to poverty; hard work makes you rich."

Nkem's experience demonstrates that when you work hard and stay committed to your goals, you can overcome difficulties and achieve your dreams. Even if others fail to recognise your efforts or if you feel inferior, perseverance and faith in God will guide you through. Nkem's journey serves as a testimony to the power of diligence and faith, urging women to strive for their best and not succumb to laziness or low self-esteem.

Lessons From Nkem

In the Book of Habakkuk, 2:3, it is written: "For the vision is yet for an appointed time; But at the end, it will speak, and it will not lie. Though it tarries, wait for it;

Because it will surely come; it will not tarry." This passage highlights the importance of patience and faith in the fulfilment of our dreams and visions.

Be vigilant about red flags in relationships and courtships, and address these issues early on rather than hoping that God will change the situation. Red flags should not be ignored, and individuals who think they are superior to others do not deserve respect. Those who seek excessive admiration and attention are often less concerned about others' feelings. Such people, sometimes idealised as "Prince Charming," are rarely caring partners.

In Ephesians 5:21-23, the Bible teaches that love and respect should be mutual in marriage. If a man loves his wife, he should not simply watch her work hard and struggle while he does nothing. If anyone must work the hardest, it should be the head of the home, as God has ordained. The man is the provider, and both should work together in harmony, not one standing by and thinking, "Let's see how you manage on your own." We should encourage and appreciate each other, ensuring that we don't let the weaker ones carry the burden alone.

Although traditionally, the man is seen as the head of the household, in today's world, both partners need to work together and support each other.

Any man who sits idly while his wife bears the burden of family responsibilities is failing in his role. The Bible states that anyone who cannot provide for their household is worse than an unbeliever. Men should prioritise their family's well-being and support their wives and children before engaging in external affairs. This principle underlines the importance of shared responsibilities and mutual respect in a marriage.

Nkem's experiences, along with these biblical teachings should encourage everyone, both believers and non-believers, to pursue their dreams while placing their trust in God. She believes that with faith and effort, dreams from childhood to maturity can be realised. As you read this book, she prays that God will enlighten your heart, guide you through life's challenges, and help you achieve your aspirations.

Remember, success is not an overnight achievement but a journey of persistence, faith, and hard work. If you do not give up, if you keep the faith and commit to working diligently towards your goals, you will find that your dreams and purpose are within reach. May this book be a source of inspiration and guidance, bringing blessings and understanding to all who read it, in the mighty name of Jesus. Amen.

www.ingramcontent.com/pod-product-compliance
Lightning Source LLC
Chambersburg PA
CBHW071225260626
47162CB00004B/1432